Brockenspectre

Caroline Moir

Brockenspectre

Caroline Moir

First published in Great Britain in 2021 by
Victorina Press
Wanfield Hall
Kingstone
Uttoxeter
Staffordshire, ST14 8QR
England

Typesetting and Layout: Jorge Vasquez
Cover Artwork: Clarrie-Anne Cooper
Editor: Amanda Huggins

British Library Cataloguing in Publication Data
A catalogue record for this book is available from the British Library.

ISBN: 978-1-9169057-2-6

Typeset in 11pt Garamond
Printed and bound in Great Britain by 4edge Ltd.

for Chris

and Kate, Rachel, and

Benedict

Grateful thanks to:

Anne Banks, Zoe Sharp, John Scott and members of Warehouse Writers and Writers Rump workshops; and Michael Schmidt MBE, Carcanet Press, and Rev'd Dr Chris Taylor; for the generosity of their time, and the quality of their editorial comments.

Brocken spectre: the magnified and detached shadow of an observer; typically on a mountain.

Endpaper

At the hotel they told me the autumn had been quiet, not the usual gales blown across from Maine on hurricane wings. Afterwards it had snowed, the most for years, they said. It had frozen, thawed, and frozen again.

Now the temperature had risen sufficiently to create a thin mist. Behind me, the low sun was a hole in the sky sinking beyond the western fells.

I couldn't resist the lure of violet shadows, the chance to plunge up to my thighs through the snow's crust, though it was a risk hiking alone in winter. I could have gone over Loughrigg, but I never knew where I was and, nervous of the ice on the steep steps down to Red Bank, I chose Silver Howe. It was always beautiful, and well-travelled. Today I'd seen no one.

I felt safer as I lost height and slowed at the sight of the juniper thicket. Before Ed enticed me to these uplands I'd not encountered juniper. The grey-blue needles were laced by spiders' webs, steely and brilliant with frost, drops of water frozen into their centres like moonstones. I wondered what secrets might be hidden under them and among the glassy, tumbled rocks of the beck.

Coming out of the thicket I saw a brockenspectre, my brockenspectre, on the other side of the ravine. It was as much a surprise as the first. My good omen I called it, before I knew what would happen. Without haloes maybe neither was a real spectre, but both were uncanny, and the legend of the witches' frolics on Walpurga's Eve granted me a glimpse into their weirdness.

The spectre stalked me, attached yet unattached. The path veered left. With each bend I watched it walk away, turn, follow me.

Its mimicry summoned you.

Summoned you, Hild. So blue and pink and silver. As a child your hair must have been almost white. You, Heddi, seducer, strife-bringer. Whatever happened to you was always a disappointment, or worse.

So unlike me. So like me. I dropped towards the wall. To recall you was dangerous – a harbinger of things to come. The spectre stole after me, separate but inevitable, and I became afraid. I crossed my fingers. I wished you and I have opposite times.

Campus

Ed rang me from his office. It was something he never did and the interruption pleased me.

'Miriam?'

'Who else?'

'Sorry.' He was harassed rather than apologetic.

'Miriam, would you like to carry on with your class after the holiday?'

My class never ran in the summer.

'Why?'

'Would you?'

'No, I've just begun to get to grips with writing–'

'It'd be a couple of hours a week.'

'And at least an hour of preparation, plus marking.'

'Not much of either. It's one student.'

One? Even a class for one was a distraction. I didn't want to teach after the holiday. I was silent.

'Thank you – you've made our academic lives a lot easier.'

'I haven't said yes, Ed.'

'Silence signifies assent.'

'Don't be an– '

He laughed. I stared at the phone. It was unthinkable for the university to put on a class for one student. Nearly five o'clock. I'd go and haul Ed from his office, tell him no, before – with his alacrity for organisation – he set things in motion. I left the flat, the concrete stairs unyielding beneath my feet. I wasn't going to do it, even if it meant giving up the extra pay, holiday money for me and Ed.

The weather vane on Old House had swung round and a north wind startled the daffodils lining the path. I scuffed through the previous year's needles under the cedar tree, tossing them from my boots. They were so dry and light they stuck to my toecaps as if they were magnetic.

At Ed's door, I put my head round chanting, '"The north wind doth blow, and we shall have snow . . ." Are you coming home?'

'I'm just about done.' He looked up. 'It isn't too late for snow.'

He went back to his computer. I lifted a mass of files from his other chair, dumped them on the floor and sat down.

'What's this about a student? I don't want to do it, Ed.'

He glanced at me, put out.

'It's one of next year's entry. We were finalising the admissions and she was standing in the doorway.'

He looked back at his screen.

'And?'

She said, '"Sorry, so sorry I'm Hild, Hild Whittaker, you wouldn't remember me, and I'm going to study for an English degree" – she meant Foundation English. Francesca said we always remembered the mature applicants–'

'How old is she?'

He cocked his head, his glasses slipping sideways, and smiled. I knew why. He thought my interest meant I had weakened. That I wasn't going to put up a struggle against what he, no, they – I had begun to understand how the college worked – wanted.

'About forty? But she seemed girlish. Francesca asked how we could help. She said she wanted to do the class for people like her who were rubbish at grammar and spelling and things.'

To say you were "rubbish" at something you were going to study was negative. No, that was too strong. It indicated need, but being made to feel I ought to help didn't make me any more willing.

'Is she rubbish?'

'If she was, she wouldn't have been offered a place. Trouble is she didn't achieve the necessary C at GCSE, and when Jeff and Francesca interviewed her last backend they told her taking the language skills course was a condition of entry. Jeff pointed out she couldn't do the class as she wasn't registered, and anyway it didn't run after Easter. She whispered something about having found a flat and got herself a job at the garden centre especially so she could do it before the autumn.' He seemed irritated. 'We could hardly hear her. She stood there looking miserable.'

'Didn't you ask her to sit down?'

'No.' His eyes dropped to his computer. He could hear the accusation in my voice. 'She caught us by surprise – and Jeff had already explained there was no course in the summer. He advised her to find private tuition. She murmured something about how she knew she was a nuisance but she was doing extra hours at the pub to help with costs as it was, and if she couldn't do the class now she might not be able to keep up, and it might not be worth her doing the degree at all.'

He started to tap at his keyboard.

'Why did she choose English if she hadn't got a C?'

'Dunno.' Other than in the motivation of his own students, Ed didn't take much interest, though he was solicitous of the wellbeing of them all.

'Jeff carried on examining the lists, and she didn't go. Didn't move. Eventually Francesca asked her to take a seat outside. When she left the room Francesca said she might countenance a class over the summer as long as we put a note on her file about the course being run in exceptional circumstances.'

Where was this going?

'I don't want to, Ed.'

'All right, but let me finish telling you. I got her back. By this time we were all standing in a sort of semi-circle. We told her what we'd arranged and she beamed, and sort of wiggled–'

'Wiggled?'

'Wriggled. I don't know. She whispered what day was the course, and she was certain the garden centre wouldn't mind changing her shifts, and then in an audible voice, "Thank you, thank you for being so good to me", and skipped out as if she'd won a prize.'

'I haven't said yes.'

The printer clunked, juddered. Ed jerked the paper. 'This is a horrible machine.' He got up and lifted his jacket from the hook behind his desk. 'No, but you will.'

'What makes you so certain?'

'You need the work.'

He was right. Even if I wanted to live with Ed, and I did, being a part-timer meant I was dependent on him. Though I didn't like being reminded of it. The only other work I might find was supply teaching and I wasn't prepared to do that.

'I thought the university was broke. How will it pay me?'

'We'll find something. For the actual contact time.'

'Given the current financial situation I'm surprised Francesca is approving it.'

'Foundation English won't be viable next year if

Hild doesn't sign on.'

'Which would put Jeff in a spot.'

His glasses flashed at me, asking me to collaborate.

'It'll stand you in good stead with the university. And with Francesca.'

He unlocked the filing cabinet, placed the document in a folder, locked it and hugged me to him.

'Trust me, Miriam, three hours a week, max.'

I woke to white light reflected onto the ceiling, scrambled out of bed and leapt across the floor.

'Whoopee! It's snowed.'

'It won't last, not this time of year.'

A precarious slice of snow balanced on the twigs and branches of the trees opposite the window.

'It must be four inches deep.'

'It'll mess up the schedule,' he said.

'You sound smug.'

'Who, me?'

'You said it wasn't too late for a snowstorm.'

Ed stretched. 'Breakfast. A walk, I think. See what the winter landscape reveals. With such students as turn up. There won't be many.'

I've never been able to ignore snow. I decided to skip work and went out into The Close. I tried to make a bird, but without legs it was a blob. In the end I made an owl. I drew the feathers in with my fingers, found a hooked twig for its beak and scraped the path for two bits of gravel for its eyes. It was uncanny, realistic, only too ready to swoop on any famished robin. It glimmered, long after the rest of the snow had melted, eerie in the shadow cast by our block of flats.

'Hild Whittaker's been to see me.'

Ed brandished an envelope in an uncertain fashion. He smelt of beer.

'Look. A letter. Don't know how she does it.'

'Does what?'

'Gets in.' He was mystified.

'Who? The student from the other day?'

'She just turned up in my office. I said I'd be a while, she said she'd wait. I forgot about her. Three quarters of an hour later Jeff rang to say he was at the pub and she was still hanging around.'

'What did she want?'

'She wanted to sort out her courses.'

'And?'

'I explained, again, there was nothing to be done until the new academic year. She whispered "sorry" and put this in my hand.'

'What does it say?'

'Don't know. Didn't open it. Met up with Jeff and had a few pints.'

'Did you get something to eat?'

'Pie.'

'We're setting off early, I'm going to pack.'

Ed followed me into the bedroom and collapsed on the bed still waving the envelope.

'Why don't you read it?'

He opened it and took out a page of squared paper torn from an exercise book. In a breathy tone he said, *"Dear Dr Gallagher"*.

'Isn't that a bit unkind?'

He sighed and read the letter. Then he scrumpled the paper and tossed it at the waste bin. It fell short.

I picked it up, smoothed it out.

'Dear Dr Gallagher,

Thank you so much for seeing me on Monday, I know it was a bit cheeky of me, coming in the holidays, but I was begining to wonder, whether I would be able, to cope with all the courses, and Gray said that if I needed, to put my mind at rest, you wouldn't mind if I came to see you which you didn't!! I have never been treated with so much consideraton as I have since I was acepted by the college and I just want to thank you, for your part, in making me feel, so welcome, and so much at home, in fact I feel more at home here, than I ever have in Leeds even though, I really did enjoy the writer's group there!! This is to wish you a very HAPPY EASTER."

'The courses were an excuse – she just wanted to come and see you.' I stuck the note beneath the lump of quartz Ed used as a paperweight, and pushed my underwear into the top flap of my case.

'You didn't say she was from Leeds.' I rolled sweaters and trousers around shoes.

'She's from Liverpool. Like a lot of us – begin somewhere and end up making our homes somewhere else.' The beer was making him solemn.

'Are you going to pack?'

'No'. He rolled himself upright, took off his glasses, dropped his clothes on the floor and flopped back into bed. I began to undress. As I removed my sweater his eyes studied me. How much did he see? I switched off the lamp. Now the room was lit solely by the light beside Ed. Was I a lovely, haloed, blur to him?

He raised his arms, 'Come here, furriner, I love you.'

Hazy. Not haloed. A foreigner. For a moment he was strange to me, this man who'd found refuge from the flatlands of Essex in the northern fells. I barely knew him.

Then I recovered the lover. I took the clasp out of my hair. Shaking it loose, I thrust back my shoulders, pulled my cami over my head, and, in homage to my origins, holding my cami taut in my two hands as if it was my partner, I strutted a tango to the bed. Ed laughed, reached for me, and tipped me under the duvet.

You didn't come to the first classes after the spring break. Ed offered to find out why, but I told him not to. It wasn't important for you to do so as yet, and your absence let me concentrate on coaching Magda and Milosz. In fact, I was thankful. I resented allowing him and Francesca to persuade me to tutor you, and I wanted you to change your mind. For your sake – it was risky beginning a university course at forty – and mine, I hoped you didn't come.

As the exams were about to begin, you turned up.

I had just finished putting an exercise on the board for Magda and Milosz, when the door opened, and you were there saying, 'I'm Hild', and repeating how lucky you were to be allowed to take this class.

The sight of you bothered me. The hair which fell below your shoulders was pure silver, with the odd thread of the palest white gold, and your eyes were such an extraordinary blue they didn't look real. I asked you to sit down. Before I could prevent it, you sat in my place at the head of the table, facing the broad Edwardian windows. I removed my books from in front of you, and seated myself beside Magda.

'What shall I do?' Your smile was cajoling.

'First, let me introduce you. Magda, Milosz, this is Hild Whittaker who is joining us, joining me, for the rest of the summer term, until she becomes a fully fledged student in the autumn.'

'Fully fledged?' Milosz enquired.

I wrote "fully fledged" and "fledgling" on the white board, explaining a fledgling was a baby bird which had not grown all its feathers.

'Fully fledged is the term for the bird having all its feathers so it can fly.'

You said, 'It's great, isn't it? Baby birds are born in the spring and get their independence in the autumn, like I will.'

The broad vowels, the a's and u's and e's, along with the half-swallowed d's and g's, made your words move, sticky in your mouth, like toffee. Magda looked confused, Milosz intent, and I saw they had difficulty in deciphering your accent.

'You know, I'll be doing my own thing. A bit late maybe, but it's never too late.'

Magda looked to me for clarification.

You were starting your foundation year, I said. For your degree you were, among other things, taking creative writing, and you might even join Jeff's, Dr Young's, writing workshop.

'It takes place in this room every fortnight in the first two semesters, Hild.'

Your face was unresponsive. Magda and Milosz looked polite, as they had done throughout my introduction. English was merely a tool for them.

'We are all fledglings – me and Magda we are fledgling Brits, and Miriam is too a fledgling,' Milosz said.

You said, 'Miriam's a funny name.'

'It's Spanish – and English – and Hebrew. And it's "is a fledgling too", Milosz, the "too" comes at the end of the sentence.'

'Why are you a fledgling, Miriam?'

'I am a fledgling writer.'

'Have you published anything?' The question was greedy.

'Miriam is writing the book of short stories about herself. It will be so good,' Magda announced.

'That's unusual, a book of short stories about you.'

'Magda means a memoir. And no, I haven't published anything.'

You were still poised on the edge of the chair. 'I write poetry and I'm writing a novel,' you said, and continued with what was unlikely to be irony, 'Fledgling Brits isn't what the people on my estate in Leeds would say about you two.'

They ignored this comment. They might not even have understood.

I signalled to them to introduce themselves.

'I am Magda Drozd.'

'And I, Milosz Drozd. We are second-year students. We do business studies. Magda comes from Romania and I from Poland.

'Going back when you've finished?'

'No. Magda and I will stay and work in the UK. That is why we are fledgling Brits.' Milosz was enjoying his newly acquired vocabulary.

'It must be lonely for you being so far from home. You must come round to our flat.'

'Our flat?' I asked. From what Ed said I assumed you were here on your own.

'Mine and Gray's.'

Magda shook her head. 'Not so lonely. At our wedding . . .' She sought my help.

'Magda and Milosz got married last summer. Their families came over. Their English friends, the town's Polish community and some of the university staff were there too.'

'It is wonderful,' Magda says, 'how many friends we had. But we like to come to you anyway?' She looked at Milosz for confirmation. He nodded.

She turned to me, 'Miriam is just to read us a bit of her story. What is it called again?'

'"*Allá Lejos*".'

You asked, 'What does it mean, a la Ley Hoss?' Your body had sunk into your chair and you seemed to be sucking in the information. I had an inkling of the voracious need which had got you to this campus.

'It's Spanish for "far away".'

'Will you read, Miriam?'

With you here, I had much rather not, but I couldn't refuse Magda, her brown eyes resting on me in unfounded belief.

. . . Today she was tempted to search for details of her secondary school. Did it survive the way she thought of it? A building of concrete and glass attached to an old house, beside it a playing field, a girl dribbling a ball with a hockey stick, next door the Polo Club. Lunch there every day. What had happened to her headmaster? And the others?

Something strange happens when you remember memories. They become memory of memory.

If she searched for the school, what might happen to her memories? Might she remember less?

If there was a possibility of remembering more she must.

She searched. Reeling past her, the pictures were like reflections in the windows of a train through which she glimpsed the present landscape.

The centenary, sports cups being given to young athletes, stage make-up painted onto young lips. Her headmaster. She always thought his name was English, but it was German. How could she not have known?

Here were classrooms. Here she was.

So long ago, she was not where she thought, in the back row, but in the second to back. She was writing. She looked so clean, so tidy, so young. Not the Miriam she remembered, who felt much older.

It was her, far away, the other side of the Atlantic, but not her.

When I finished reading there was a moment of quiet, then Magda said, 'It is difficult to go from home. Milosz and me we can go back. Why you cannot go back, Miriam?'

'I can, I suppose. I have a brother there – but no home now.'

'It is very far, very *lejos*,' Milosz smiled. 'And expensive to get.'

'It's not about your home, is it?' Your accent was even stronger, thicker, than before.

I wasn't sure of your meaning, or if I wanted to know what you meant. I decided not to discuss it. I asked Magda and Milosz to do their exercise.

I turned to you, 'Write me something about yourself, Hild – how you came to be here, why you want to be here – so I can assess your weaknesses and strengths.'

You looked sidelong at me and mumbled, 'I don't want to write about myself, my life's not interesting.'

'To get to university as a mature student has to be interesting.'

You looked uncomfortable and didn't reply.

After a few seconds I gave in. 'All right. Why don't you retell a story?'

Nothing. 'A myth? A legend? I need to know how you handle language.'

Reluctantly you picked up your biro. I watched as you worked on an unlined sketchpad. Your writing sloped down and down until you were out of space, leaving the left corner blank. In it you inscribed, "By Hild Whittaker".

You handed it to me. 'This is the best I can do. I'm sure I can't write as well as you, Miriam.'

I felt uneasy, but I didn't know why.

You had chosen to retell a fairy story, Cinderella. The narrative ran on in a breathless rush, littered with misplaced commas. This was far worse than your letter to Ed. How on earth had they allowed you in?

'It's vivid, Hild, but the punctuation needs sorting.'

Your smile dragged from you by the presence of Magda and Milosz, your voice wobbling, you said, 'I'm rubbish at full stops and commas and things.'

Paragraphing and apostrophes could wait. I started to explain the reason for full stops, but you didn't listen. Instead, you stared around the room, lingering on the three replicas of Della Robbia Madonnas nailed above the picture rail. When Old House was a boarding school, Thornthwaite Room had been used for dining and recreation. Had the three virgins looked as incongruous presiding over the bicker of the girls as they did over our students? Then you looked out of the window.

'There's Dr Young. He's head of English,' you exclaimed. After a pause. 'And Dr Gallagher. The student mentor.'

Jeff and Ed were weaving their way through clumps of students who drifted across the patchy lawn in front of Old House, carrying coffees whose stability was threatened by the tug of their rucksacks and bags. How did you know Ed had been given the task of being student mentor? It had only just happened. As Francesca put it in one of her recent evasive speeches as Dean, "driven by the financial strain of the university", she had taken "an upcoming retirement as an opportunity to reallocate the pastoral roles of the campus staff." What else did you know – that Ed was my partner?

'Shall we go on?'

'I'm easily distracted. I know it's stupid, but Gray says it's how I get my ideas.'

'Not stupid, Hild, never say you are stupid. Next time why don't you sit with your back to the window?'

I sounded bossy to my ears, but your smile was vague, as if you hadn't understood.

'One of the best ways to learn to punctuate is to read your work aloud.'

'I can't.'

'Why? What you've written is good.'

'I won't.' You gave Milosz and Magda a quick look.

Perhaps we were sitting too close. 'Do you want to move further away?'

There was no response. Taking your pad, I shifted down the table and beckoned to you, aware I was behaving as if you were a school pupil. You got up and followed me with lumpen obedience.

I hesitated. 'Shall I read it? And you tell me where to put the punctuation?'

Was that a nod or a shake of your head? I began to read.

'"One day a coach had drawn up outside their beautiful sunken garden where, Ellie used to play hide and seek, with her daddy"'

I looked at you, expecting you to suggest a full stop. You didn't look at me. I had made a mistake. I wasn't able to force words from you. You weren't going to do what I asked. Now there was nothing to be done except carry on reading to a mutinous you.

'"The coachman got down and came over to where,

Ellies daddy was standing searching around, for Ellie who was hidden behind a bush, and said he was terribly sorry one of their horses, had gone lame and the mistress, had sent to ask if she and her three daughters could beg, a lodging for the night as it was too late to go on that evening, they were going to Scarborough, her daddy was such a kind man he said, yes and called to Ellie come out because they had people, come and Ellie came out, and held on to his hand as the lady, came down from the coach followed by three little girls but, they were all bigger than her, and they stayed the night and Ellies daddy, had a good time. Ellie hadn't heard him laugh so much for ever. Ellies daddy said maybe we'll go to Scarborough ourselves, And so they all went to Scarborough later that year, Ellies daddy married the lady from the coach and the three girls were bridesmaids, and Ellie was her daddys, page boy and her hair was cut like a boy, by Ellies stepmother, and that was the last time she was happy because, after that Ellies stepmother kept, being rude and aggressive to Ellie telling Ellies daddy she was a bad girl and she was made to do the kitchen, work and sleep in the cinders but they were too hot and she was called Cinderella."

I looked up. 'Did you enjoy hearing your story?'

The way you sat resisted me. I knew I should try to get you to respond – the fundamental rule of teaching is establish who is in charge – but this was the first time we'd met and I thought it might be unfair. Besides, you weren't going to answer. I wondered if, like giving Magda and Milosz so many details of your upcoming course, in reading your work to you, I had gone too far. I gave in again. I handed the sheet of paper back to you, and said, 'That's it for today. Milosz, Magda, give me yours and I'll go over them this evening. See you next week.'

Milosz went to the door, but Magda stayed by the

table. She smiled at you. 'Do you want to come with us, Hild? We go to the canteen.'

You stood up. 'Yes, yes, I'd like it very much, thank you for asking me.'

I watched them go, Milosz in the lead, Magda with you. Your body had regained its youth and lightness. It had a sexuality which combined the mature with the immature. Or to be more exact, the knowing with the immature. Was I right? Were you immature? Ed said I was perceptive. Simon had said it too. Only, as he became embroiled in his affair and my comments were sharper, he said my perceptiveness was a weapon, and the term became less a compliment in his mouth, more an insult.

I left the Thornthwaite Room and crossed through the Library, reflecting on what you'd written. It was unusual. I expected a straight retelling, enough to give me the necessary information about what you should work on. Instead I had been offered a point of view. Jeff said your language was fresh, but it was childish. "Ellie" was a diminutive. Good daddy, stepmother, Ellie badly treated. The conventional elements were there, but there was no prince, no ball, the cinders were too hot to be slept in. It was about a family, a domestic, not fairy, tale, unless hidden within the daddy was Ellie's prince. Why had you chosen to make the Cinderella so young? Aside from the gush of story onto the paper, the writing disclosed something nasty and punitive. The stepmother punishing Cinderella for being the father's child? It was one interpretation of the story, but your account felt more as if you were offering me a clue to who you were. I had to be careful with you.

Hild

She's tall and thin and her hair's brown sort of streaky blond brown and her eyes are a funny colour like green olives, but dark. Jeff, Dr Young, says I've to keep a journal it will be good for my writing keep it going like riding a bicycle so I am writing down everything that happens and what I think. When I came in to the seminar room today, the Thornthwaite room that's what they call the room where she teaches, it isn't hers it's used by lots of people I know because I looked at the timetable pinned on the door but she seems to think it's hers, she was with two other people young, not like her she's quite a bit older than me. She looked at me as if she was surprised, I don't know why she knew I was coming, even though I missed the class the previous week because I wanted to see something of where we were living and we'd gone on the bus to Carlisle. Gray said the Carlisle people sounded as if they were from Newcastle, but I wouldn't know, we've never really been to Newcastle even though Gray's mum and dad were Geordies because his mum was dead and his dad came to visit us specially after we had Tanya because it was easier than us getting up there with a baby.

Anyway then she said in that posh voice of hers though she's got a funny way of saying things that have r in them she was Miriam, Miriam Henderson my tutor for the summer and she asked me to sit down so I sat in the chair at the head of the table because it was empty, well it had some papers in front of it but there was no one sitting in it. Anyway it was her chair not that any of the chairs belonged to anyone really, because she came and took her papers away and sat beside the girl who she called Magda and introduced me to Magda and Milosz, who it turned out was Magda's husband and came from Poland though he looked like half the men round here. And she told me about them getting married and then she told them about me, what I was going to be doing in September when the uni starts properly for me. She told them about me doing English and creative writing and I don't mind people knowing what I am doing as Gray says I am very easy to get on with because I find it easy to chat to people and people like to chat to me. They talk to me about themselves a lot which is funny really because I'm quite private about me and I didn't think she should have said right off what I was doing she should have left me to tell them. Anyway then she made me write and she wanted me to write about how I got to uni at my age which I thought was cheek, I'd got there because my lecturer in Leeds thought I was really good and I should go to uni but I couldn't get into Leeds uni and anyway I hate Leeds. So instead I wrote about Cinderella but I didn't tell the story the usual way because it would be boring I wrote it the way I thought about it, the way my life makes me see Cinderella, about how much she was loved by her daddy but how the step mother and the step sisters got between her and her daddy. My lecturer in Leeds would have said how interesting the story was he was really encouraging. I said I knew it wouldn't be as good as what she wrote, she's writing about her life in short stories, she told Magda it was a memoir, but she didn't say anything except it needed punctuation and then she tried to make me read it out loud but I wouldn't I knew it would be rubbish because I was in a hurry, so she read it out loud to me putting in the full stops as she did so. It sounded good but it was embarrassing. At the end she asked me if I liked hearing it read out loud but I didn't answer and she didn't go on and just said to Magda and Milosz to give her their work and she'd give it back the next week. Then Magda said they were going to the canteen and would I like to go and I was really pleased because it meant I'd started to make friends already even though I wasn't actually a student until September. And it showed her that I could make friends I didn't need her to introduce me and all. She thinks she's interesting because she's half foreign or something but I'll bet she hasn't had a life like I've had. My lecturer in Leeds said my life was horrifying and fascinating in equal measure.

Class

You weren't at the next session, official for you, *pro bono* for Magda and Milosz. Ed wanted to contact you to insist you came to class, but as I was only being paid for the sessions at which you were present he didn't have the authority. Non-attendance was something he and Francesca had not thought about.

The following week, Magda and Milosz were caught up in their exams, and as I waited I was on my own. After thirty minutes I gave up and decided to go to the Co-op for bread.

Rounding the corner into the aisle which contained household goods, I met you head on.

'Hild.'

Silence.

'I missed you in class.'

'Was it – I was twenty minutes late.'

'I waited for half an hour.'

'Sometimes I don't get the time right.'

Your eyes had become round. They had lost their blue. The colour was real. They slid away from mine and examined the detergents.

'It doesn't matter too much, we can catch up. How are things going?

'Good.' You fidgeted with your mobile, picked up a bottle of detergent. 'I've got to go, Miriam. To get tea.'

You hurried to the till.

When I got to the flat I contemplated my unexpected extra hour. I had set aside the piece I was writing about my mother – it was too difficult – and there was not enough time to settle to other work. I'd get our supper. I started the preparations, took onions, garlic, tomatoes and parsley out of the fridge and began to chop them up for sauce. Had you forgotten the class, or were you late? Either way, why not tell the truth?

The front door opened, there was a thud as he dropped his bag, and Ed came into the kitchen. 'Listening to Jacques Brel, the lonely flatlander?'

'He's a poet, flatlander yourself.'

It was an old tease. Ed ought to have been sympathetic to Brel, but he wasn't. He loved country music. He said it was about the rhythm, but I thought it was nostalgia for the America he lost when Laura left him and took Tom back to be raised as an American.

He opened the fridge and examined inside. 'Had a good day?'

I pulled the baguette from its paper. 'Quite. You?'

He looked at the bread. 'So-so. Been into town?'

'How do you think I got this?' I flourished the stick at him.

'What time?'

'Time?' I placed the baguette on the counter.

'What time did you go into town?'

I put my fists on my hips. 'Ed, is this an inquisition?'

He smiled, shook his head.

'It was around four. Hild didn't show. Why do you want to know?'

'She turned up in my office.'

'Your office? When?'

'About five. In tears. Said she was sorry, she'd been a bit late, and you'd not been there and she hoped she hadn't done anything wrong. Said it was a privilege for her to have someone 'like Miriam' teach her, you were such an intelligent lady and she hoped you wouldn't be cross.'

Did you intend to mollify me?

'I met her in the shop at four – she was off to make her tea.' I ran water into the pasta pan. 'I waited for half an hour. Wait thirty minutes and go. University rules, okay?'

'I suppose so.' He broke the end off the baguette and chewed on it. 'I had her happy, finally. I invited her and her husband – Graham? – to the do tomorrow night.'

'Inflicting the Founder's Day lecture on them? "The Landscape of the Lakes". How is it possible you are using the same title as last year? Or do you have to economise on titles as well?'

Ed grinned. 'They'll enjoy it – and you'll get to meet Graham.'

'I wasn't going to go.'

'Why not? Nicole is bound to be there. You'd like to see her. What are you making for tea?'

'Pasta and salad. And bread.'

'Carbs. My favourite. Just like you.'

His glasses pushed up like goggles, he stepped towards me, ready to wrap his body around me.

'Ed, Hild said she was twenty minutes late, and when I said I'd been there for half an hour she said she doesn't always know the time – but she's got her mobile.'

He kissed me, dropped his hands from my shoulders and picked a grape from the bowl.

'She's disorganised? Are you doing anything later?'

He tossed the grape in the air, caught it in his mouth, crunched it, swallowed it.

'Carrying on with the piece for my kids. Turning it into short stories, like you suggested. '

The subject went no further. I hadn't told the

children about Simon's affair, so they held Ed responsible and had nothing to do with him. It hurt him. It was easier with me and Tom. The split between Ed and Laura happened earlier than that between me and Simon. In any case Tom was younger and I was slotted away on a different continent and didn't have to be taken into account.

'Can I help with tea?'

I looked at Ed, blocking the corridor which passed for a kitchen. The staff quarters were skimped. Square rooms with low ceilings. There was hardly enough space for two. How had they managed when there were three of them in the flat?

'Nothing much, unless you want to grate the cheese. Stay and talk to me.'

'Need to check my emails.'

'You've– '

He disappeared into Tom's old room, where our laptops stood facing each other on regulation desks. Ed spent so much time working. So much more than at the beginning. "The Landscape of the Lakes". When we met – tramping the Devon shore at our respective conferences on landscape and language and igneous geology – his enthusiasm for the Lake District, for this isolated rural campus, captivated me. For the first time I found myself excited by rocks. Which was why a twice used title was disappointing.

'It's ready.' I carried the bowls of spaghetti into the living room and laid them at the end of the dining table unencumbered by Ed's paperwork.

'Hild's sent me an email.'

I pushed the parmesan and the pepper mill towards him.

'She says she's stopped feeling worthless.'

'Isn't that an overreaction on her part? Missing each

other was unfortunate, but not disastrous.'

I twirled spaghetti into my spoon. 'Does she know we are partners?'

'Don't know. Probably not. I haven't mentioned it. Have you?'

'No.'

The following Thursday you were waiting for me outside the Library. Your hair shone in the sun and you had on an old-fashioned frock, sprigged with forget-me-nots which matched your eyes.

'What a lovely dress, Hild. Where did you get it?'

'Made it when Tanya was little.'

So, like me, you had at least one child. 'I can't sew at all.'

'Didn't you have to at school?'

'No. It wasn't that kind of school.'

We went through the Library to the Thornthwaite Room. I opened the door. At the start of what was about to be a glorious summer, five months of it, the room was close and stale. The frock altered your behaviour, feminised you. Infantilised you. You scurried to the window and struggled with the latch in an ineffectual fashion until I rescued you.

'It's a special lock, Hild. Let me.'

Flushing, you said, 'I'm no good at these kinds of things,' but persisted in trying to raise the sash.

Between your efforts and mine it became a scuffle, until you flung away, saying, 'It was stupid of me to try. You do it, you know how to do it.'

'Not stupid, Hild, you mustn't say you're stupid, you're just not used to the building. All the ground floor windows have these kinds of locks. According to Francesca Farrington it keeps out "undesirables".'

'Undesirables?'

'Tramps, gypsies. The homeless. They get very worried by gypsies round here.'

'Are there many of them?'

'Once a year, yes. There's a horse fair at Appleby.'

Was I reassuring you that you had done nothing wrong? I didn't know, but I wished you'd leave me to deal with my own classroom.

'We'd a lot of undesirables where we lived in Leeds. Druggies. Don't know how me and Gray kept Tanya off them. We did, but I'm glad we've moved. It's nice. Quiet.'

'People take drugs here too.'

'Yeah, but not like on our estate. Druggies and dogs. Big ones. That's all there was.'

In order to have the blinds open without distracting you I sat you with your back to the window. I gave you a paragraph from a story, and asked you to replace the punctuation I had removed. You did this, and when we went through the passage well over four fifths of the sentences were right.

It was too hot with the sun full on us, but it was a shame to keep it out. We moved side-on to the window, me sitting between you and it to block some of your sightline. Why did I feel it was it necessary to behave like this? The next exercise – inserting punctuation as you read aloud – you also did well. Your reading was fluent and expressive. Your technical skills were far less poor than I'd been expecting. Maybe your mistake-ridden Cinderella was due to the effect of nervousness.

Then you ran your finger under a sentence. 'I wouldn't put a full stop there if I was the writer, so what does it matter?'

'Well, if you want the meaning to be as clear as

possible . . .'

'But every reader reads something different. The lecturer in Leeds said.'

'Not entirely, you couldn't have common agreement. If a recipe for making a cake had a full stop in the wrong – '

'It wouldn't matter. If the handwriting's rubbish, like mine, the cake might turn out rubbish. If I got a comma wrong it wouldn't matter.'

'Don't say your work is rubbish, Hild, you undermine yourself. If you're going to write well you've got to get the– '

'It's my writing. What it means to me. That's what's important.'

Your mouth shut tight and you stared past my shoulder. I looked round. There was nothing to see except the level, somnolent lawn. In one week the trees had grown up, had stopped being frivolous.

As at our first session, you refused to respond. As at our first session, after a couple of minutes, I gave in.

'If that's how you feel, Hild, and as you don't seem to need to work on punctuation as much as I expected, why don't we have a go at essay writing? In the long run it might be the most useful thing to do.'

'I've learned how to do essays.'

'Yes, but it's a bit more complicated at university. Why don't you write an essay on any author you like? It doesn't have to be long – a thousand words. An introduction, two or three main ideas, a conclusion.'

'Dr Young said I had to work on the basics.'

'Jeff Young might argue that writing a good essay was a basic.'

You sat there, stubborn. Despite the open window the air was heavy and thick.

I tried again. 'Please, Hild, bring me in an essay next

week so we can work on those skills.'

'I didn't think I had to do assignments. This isn't a real class anyway. You're only getting paid if I come.'

'How do you know?'

'I heard Dr Gallagher and Dr Farrington discussing it.'

'Despite what Ed – Dr Gallagher – and Dr Farrington said about money, it is a real class, and as you want to complete it before September–'

Your voice quavered. 'I haven't got time to do an essay. I'm working three nights a week as well as the days.'

'All right, over the next week read a novel – you can do the analysis here. Do you want me to recommend one?'

'I can find a book for myself.'

'Hild's been to see me.'

We were eating supper, when Ed announced this. I wondered why he'd kept it to himself since he came in.

'And?'

'She says you're doing things she can already do, and you said she was no good at writing.'

'That's –' I stopped, controlling myself.

A blatant lie. Forcing me to back down over the punctuation I just about accepted, but saying I was overly critical? I didn't understand why you'd made what was as good as an outright accusation.

I continued. 'A little harsh? Not quite true? I didn't say she wasn't good at writing. I gave her some paragraphs to punctuate, which she did well. She went on about punctuation being a personal matter. She was almost hostile, as if I was – '

'Maybe she thought you were a bit dismissive?'

'I didn't want to argue about it. I told her it might be better if we looked at essay writing. I asked her to do one for next week.'

'So?'

'She said she hadn't got time. Ed, this isn't going well. She didn't come to the course when you arranged, she's skipped two sessions, she doesn't like me correcting her, and she won't do anything during the week.'

I looked at Ed as he forked rice into his mouth. Why didn't he reply? Because he was considering what to say? Sometimes I thought he was too considered, and yet when I removed his glasses, his eyes, with their short thick fringe of lashes, were unguarded, and he seemed vulnerable.

I didn't want to go on with your sessions, but I knew I shouldn't lose the possibilities tutoring you might bring, and it stopped me telling him you'd said it wasn't a proper class because I wasn't being paid. Nor did I ask why you always went to see him, and not Jeff, who was head of English, whose department you would be in when you enrolled.

Ed laid down his knife and fork. 'What are you going to do?'

'Me? I don't think it's my problem. Surely it is yours. And Jeff's. What did you say when she complained?'

Ed stood up, pushed his chair back. 'She wasn't complaining. She was upset. I told her you were a conscientious teacher and would focus on what you thought would be most useful to her. I told her she was . . .'

I knew Ed's response was professional, but it was irritating. What about my view?

'What did you tell her she was?'

'Perfectly able.'

'What did she say?'

'She wanted to get the course done before she started her studies, but your criticising has made her think she's not good enough.'

'But I haven't criticised her. I praised what was correct and explained what was incorrect.'

Ed crumpled his napkin, threw it onto his plate and hurried out of the room.

'I'm going to be late. Student-staff committee meeting. Did she agree to do anything?'

'I've asked her to read a novel– '

'Tell me when I get back, should be by half-nine.'

'I'll sort the supper things. All right?'

'Sorry. Kiss it better. Later.'

'Kiss my ass,' I shouted back. I wasn't joking, but his laughter funnelled up, its volume doubled by the emptiness of the stairs.

I closed the door to the flat at the same moment as he crashed the front door behind him. One day he'd slam it too hard and the glass would separate from its warped metal frame – but he'd never notice, too busy to be aware of surroundings other than the fells.

Ed said your refusal to borrow a novel, or be given a title, was not a rejection of my position or of me. It suggested you had initiative and independence, both of which you must possess to have got here. I granted you initiative, but I thought your independence might be partly wilfulness, and although I knew it was trivial, your refusal rankled.

The book you chose was *Of Mice and Men.* It cost you ninety pence from a charity shop. You said you might have got one cheaper somewhere else, but you preferred to do good wherever possible. Did you find it in a charity shop? It might have been a set text from your school days. If it was, and you kept it, the need it showed shamed me.

Clearly in good spirits, you left me to struggle to open the window. While I was doing so you chatted in a way

I hadn't experienced before, telling me you put the change from the pound into the box by the till.

'I always do, not usually ten pence, but pennies. It's stupid keeping a penny. When I was working at the chippy in Leeds– '

'Nice chips?'

All I intended was keeping the chat light, but your look implied I'd said something strange, as if it wasn't possible for me to know what chips were like in Leeds. Or maybe, they couldn't be nice in *her* Leeds.

'No, the fat stank halfway down the street, it was that stale, but we got them cheap. That's when I got chubby. I used to be really slim.'

'You're not chubby, Hild.'

'Well cuddly is what Gray calls me. Not like you Miriam, you're very thin for your height.'

You paused then went on, 'The kids used to chuck their pennies on the pavement outside the chip shop and I picked them up and put them in the hospice box we had on the counter. I don't know how they could waste their money like that.'

When I turned back to the room you'd placed yourself in my chair facing the window.

'It's lovely sitting here. I can see what's going on.'

There was nothing to be done. 'I hope you'll be able to concentrate.'

'You sound like my English teacher at school.' You said this with your cajoling smile, but your words made me squirm.

'It's possible. I've taught French and Spanish, and English as a foreign language.'

'So you're not like Dr Gallagher and Dr Young?'

'No. I'm temporary staff. I get paid for certain

courses – like yours. When you turn up.'

You dropped your head and your hair swung forward, hiding your face. There was a long silence which I was beginning to think was your trade-mark, but I knew this time it was my fault and hoped I hadn't destroyed the chance of a productive session.

'Which aspect of the novel do you want to look at?'

Your voice emerged muffled from behind your hair. 'Aspect?'

'The bit of the novel you're interested in.'

Your answer was swift. 'The treatment of Curley's wife and the girls down in the flophouse.'

I thought for a minute. 'I suppose you could discuss whether the stereotypical attitude to women undermines the novel's worth.'

Your raised your head and your face reappeared. You looked at me, 'What do you mean?'

'Ask yourself what the novel would be like if there had been more ordinary women in it.'

You pondered this for a few minutes. Then you said, 'They are ordinary, aren't they, for the time and the place? It's people who don't know what's ordinary who would say they weren't.'

It was a bit garbled, but Jeff was right, you had an ability to analyse.

'All right, do you want to think about the relationship between Lenny and George?'

My suggestion, to my surprise, was accepted and, the novel open at your side, you began to write. You were still using the sketch pad, or its replacement. As you worked I watched students surge from the main teaching block, their final exam over. They spread out, calling to each other. Some crashed full length onto the grass, stretching arms and flexing wrists and fingers. Did the noise and movement disrupt you? Your head lifted, but your eyes did not stray to the lawn. You asked if I had a dictionary and I went and got one from the Library. You looked something up and resumed writing.

So I was one of those who didn't know what was ordinary. Like your response to my remark about the chips, it disturbed me. It was an accusation. Had my life not been ordinary? Studying, teaching, marriage, children. Wasn't it what everyone did? What I had done. The only thing out of the ordinary was it wasn't what I'd intended.

After an hour you put your biro down. 'It looks better when it's done on the computer.'

'Yes, but it's not its looks which count, and there's nothing to stop you bringing in a laptop.'

'I can't afford one.'

'Maybe when autumn comes . . . Shall I read it now – we've got some time left?'

'No, I'll get it off of you next week when you've read it. Are you going to show it to Dr Gallagher?'

'I'll show it to Dr Young. He'll be your English lecturer.'

'I thought you'd be seeing Dr Gallagher. Will you show it to him as well?'

'If you want.'

'Are you going to get married?'

'What?'

'To Dr Gallagher. He's divorced, isn't he?'

'Yes he is. And no I'm not.'

I was disconcerted. How did you know about me and Ed? Neither of us had said anything.

Almost as if you had heard my thoughts, you answered my question. 'The ladies in Reception were talking about you and him.'

Apart from being stunned by your directness, I was taken aback to find Ed and I were being discussed. Even more, I was taken aback to find you were already on such close terms with Reception – had you been haunting the place? Why? I was gripped by a desire to know what Reception had said, but you didn't offer further comment and I couldn't bring myself to ask.

'See you next week, Miriam.' You went off with the same buoyancy which Ed described you having at your first appearance, and which I saw when you were taken to the canteen by Magda and Milosz.

As teaching was over for the year, and no one scheduled in Thornthwaite after me, I decided to stay and mark your essay. I liked the room. It was peaceful, and I didn't want to return to the flat, which I found claustrophobic in the summer, to read what I was sure was a predictable and weak bit of work.

I was wrong. It wasn't weak. Nor was it predictable. You showed insight and your punctuation was nothing like it was in your first piece. Apostrophes were a bit erratic, but commas and full stops were correct. Reading it, I wondered why I was teaching you at all. Indeed, why Jeff had insisted on your taking the class as a prerequisite to your entry. I guessed he'd been made cautious, singed by earlier failures. I marked some mistakes, made a couple of comments designed to extend your thinking, and finished with one on the overall quality. The essay was much more than satisfactory. I hoped this might encourage you and convey to you I thought you had ability. From the start I'd found you awkward to handle and I wasn't sure I liked you, but I never intended to upset you. I didn't know how it had happened.

My remarks must have pleased you. I received a note in

your inconsistent handwriting, asking for an extra tutorial to discuss the essay and the books it would be helpful to cover over the summer. The slight shock came in your postscript. If I wanted I could go round to yours, or you could come to me.

I didn't want to go and see you, but I was uncertain about you coming to see me. It might muddle the tutor-student boundary. Plus, before you settled to writing your essay you had told me about your studio, with its sofa bed, table, two chairs, gas hob and mini-fridge. I anticipated feeling guilt at your envy of our flat, small, yet, even though after two years we hadn't yet sorted out a bookcase for my books, more comfortable than yours. I asked Ed. He said if Magda and Milosz came to our place when they wanted to check things with me, why not you? There could be no harm, especially as you were not yet enrolled. I wasn't persuaded. Sometimes Ed's reasoning didn't convince me, but I overrode my misgivings and told you I'd be happy for you to come any day after I'd finished work.

You looked round the entrance to the flats with a doubtful expression. This was not what you expected.

'It's like where we were when we first went to Leeds.'

'Probably the same period – sixties?'

You didn't answer. Was this because you didn't know whether the block you lived in was built in the 1960s, or that you didn't feel the need to reply?

I brought you into the living room. Immediately you asked to see the rest of the flat.

I was at a loss. I wanted to say no, yet didn't know how to do so and remain polite. I showed you around, feeling you alert beside me. You took in everything – the narrow kitchen, the second bedroom used as an office, the outsize duvet on our bed. Back in the living room you inspected Ed's ramshackle heap of papers on the dining table. I'd attempted to tidy them before you came, but achieved nothing much more than shuffling them together.

'What a lot of paper. Are they Dr Gallagher's?' You were admiring and a little scandalised.

'Yes. Do you want some tea?'

'Thanks.'

'How's the reading going?'

'Fine.' It was an automatic rejoinder, you were not with me. Your eyes examined the pictures, the curtains, the sofa, Ed's chair, the television, my books which lined the wall under the window.

I didn't know what effect this scrutiny was having on you. Were you intimidated? Were you surprised by the furniture? I had been. White leather sofa and armchairs. It was an out-of-character choice for Ed. Probably it had been Laura's. He hadn't said, and now, under your unashamed appraisal – there was nothing furtive in it, you weren't abashed by your curiosity – I realised I had failed to ask. It led me to examine the flat too. It became both very alien and very familiar. It was nothing like the sunny brick terrace of my marriage. Shadowed by the trees outside, it reminded me of the house I had lived in as a child, shuttered to keep out the heat.

'Not very colourful, is it? And not very good for a boy.'

I knew what you meant because it had been my first reaction too, but how did you know about Tom?

'Or a dog.'

Who had told you about Tom's dog?

'I never had a pet. I can't, it sets off my asthma. It's why I never smoked, not even when I first met Gray when he was working in Durham. It's why I won't let Gray smoke indoors.'

'Did you want a dog? Did it make you sad not being able to have a pet?'

'My dad said they cost too much. You have one?'

Did your question imply disapproval? Why did you always make me on edge, always afraid I had said or was about to say something wrong?

'Yes. A dog. It became too difficult to keep. My father sent it away.'

'Where?'

'Up country.'

'I guess Dr Gallagher likes you because you're foreign.'

You were trespassing on my, our, privacy. 'I have a British passport.'

'Your mum and dad here?'

'They're dead, Hild, I said as much in the first class. They never returned to England.'

'Do you wish you hadn't?'

I was reluctant to reveal myself to you, but I said, 'Occasionally.'

'I never want to be back in Liverpool.' This was stated with a sprightliness which at the same time revealed and glossed over something awful in your life.

You carried on with your examination of me. 'It must have been nice, growing up somewhere exotic.'

'It didn't seem exotic.'

I had made the tea by now, and you stirred sugar into your cup and watched the liquid swirl round and round.

'What was it like?' You were impatient, as if I were someone you knew well, a member of your family, who wasn't reacting as they ought.

I didn't know what gave you the right to assume intimacy, to feel you had the right to know about me, but I didn't know how to deny you.

'Well, the playground of my primary school didn't have tarmac, it was sand. There was no green, but there were eucalyptus trees.'

You waited.

'We used sheets of the bark for sending secret messages.'

You sipped your tea, satisfied. This was the detail you wanted – not the description of a place, but an action which gave you entry into understanding me.

'My school didn't have green either. The playground was on the roof, four floors up. There was a brick wall with a barbed wire fence on top of it, all round. To stop people falling off.'

Your experience trumped mine.

'Do you want to talk about the essay?'

'Yes, okay.'

The discussion revealed my mistake. Trying to boost, maybe placate, you, I had praised you a bit too highly, and despite your intelligence you had an inadequate notion of how much you had to learn. We looked at the reading list for Jeff's course. I asterisked the essential books, and then got up to make more tea. As I came back in you picked up Tom's birthday card to Ed. By the casual way you handled it I was sure you'd read it while I was in the kitchen.

'Is it Ed's birthday?'

'No, it's been there since last August – he hasn't got around to filing it.'

'I'll send him one this year. What's the date? When's yours?'

How could I get out of telling you?

'August the eighth, and mine is in October.'

'So is mine. We might share a party.'

Your titter sounded as if you were frightened I might reject the idea, but your next remark disproved it.

'It would have to be here, my studio is too small.'

I was astounded. 'This flat's small too.'

You gazed round and didn't appear to agree. Then you laid down Tom's card and plucked the photo of my parents from the shelf above the radiator. It had been taken outside our villa. You studied it.

'Who are they?'

'My mother and father.'

'They don't look like people usually do in photos.'

'What do you mean?'

'They don't look friendly. They aren't smiling. They aren't looking at me.'

'They didn't know they were being photographed.'

'Who photographed them?'

'My brother.'

You went on staring at their faces. 'When did he take it?'

'Just after I left to come to England, before he went to work on an *estancia*.'

I sat down in Ed's armchair, willing you to go, willing Ed home, while you continued in possession of the sofa. It was well past eight. Your eyes changed colour again. Their blue was arctic, their gleam mesmerising. I knew I should switch on the lamp, but it was behind me and I didn't want to turn away from you. I didn't know what it was you wanted, but you held the photo avidly, as if you were absorbing my parents through your fingertips, and I understood the superstition that photographs steal the soul.

After what seemed a long, long while you said,

'When's Ed coming?'

'Not for ages, he's gone to Malham Cove, on a field trip.'

There was another long emptiness, until you said, 'What time is it?' Now your voice was so light it gave the impression you were hardly present in the room.

'It must be about nine o'clock. Won't Graham be wondering where you are?'

'Yes.'

I got to my feet. 'You must go.'

You stood up. Then you lunged forward, gasping, 'I'm frightened. Hold me.'

I put my hand out, but somehow you missed it and instead made a convulsive clutch at my arm as I guided you to the door. There, I switched on the ceiling light. You were on the verge of hysteria and I seized your hand with some force so I could lead you down the stairs.

At the bottom, you freed yourself from me. I wanted to know what had panicked you, but you said, in a polite, conversational tone, 'I meant to ask when I first came. What's through the other door?'

'A communal garden for the staff flats. It's called The Close.'

You gave me a brilliant smile, said, with a gracious air, 'Thanks for the tea,' and left.

Unnerved, I returned to the flat and turned on all the rest of the lights, I didn't want any more shadows. I was confused. How did you go from hypnotising me, to near-collapse, to behaving as if nothing had happened?

It was past eleven when Ed returned and I had gone to bed. 'Hi, sweetie, sorry I'm late.' He began to check his next day's meetings on his phone. 'What have you been up to?'

'Hild came round.'

'How was she?'

'All right.'

'You don't seem too sure.'

'She was . . . If she had been a school pupil I'd have said she was impudent. We both have birthdays in October. She proposed we should share a party. Here.'

He laughed and pulled his T-shirt over his head, but I didn't know what he found funny.

'And?'

'I said the flat was too small. She shouldn't have come, Ed. It's not the same as having Milosz and Magda. She interrogated me about my parents. She didn't leave. She only went when she found out it was going to be much later before you came home. She was waiting for you.'

'I've no interest in Hild except as a student, Miriam.'

'I know – but has it occurred to you she might be very interested in you? She was inquisitive about the flat, its suitability for children – Tom – and dogs – Tom's dog.'

'But she also asked about you. You're a role model for her.'

'Not a good one.'

'Don't, Miriam, you're a great teacher and a wonderful– '

He checked himself. I suspected he was about to say "wife", forgetting I was not. A question I had been trying to avoid was becoming more urgent. I wanted to belong when I came over to study, but where had I belonged when I was with Simon? Where did I belong now?

Hild

I didn't go next time – I like Magda, she's sweet and she says funny things because she doesn't know English very well and Milosz is also very nice, but I didn't want them hearing her being bossy to me, and I didn't know they weren't going to be there. After all I'm an adult and it takes quite a lot to get to uni at my age – not that I am old, or Gray either. Gray said I ought to go to her class, he said I needed to keep on the right side of the university but I said they had to expect someone of my age to be independent. He was off on his rounds he's got a job delivering posh bread with a bakery, he couldn't get a job in a garage, he didn't try he says he's out of date it's too long since he had one. So he wasn't around when it was time for my class and he didn't know I hadn't gone. I went to the Co-op to get some things and to have a chat to Anna who works there and I ran face to face into her. She was waving one of those bageutte sticks around and talking to herself as if she was a crazy and she stopped and she asked me where I'd been at the class. So I said I'd gone there and she wasn't there, I'd been twenty minutes late, sometimes I forget the time when I'm writing and things, and she said she waited for half an hour and I hadn't gone. She said it didn't matter, but I thought she might complain to Dr Farrington or Dr Young so I thought if I went to see Dr Gallagher because he'd arranged the class, and explained that I'd been late and I didn't want to upset her because she was such a good teacher it would be a good thing. So I said I had to make Gray's tea, which I didn't it was an excuse and went up to see Dr Gallagher, in his office in the main administration building which is all glass and wooden floors, must have cost a packet. He said not to worry these things happen sometimes but as I didn't want to have to do the class in the autumn as I would be full time then try and remember to turn up. Set an alarm he said to remind you to go. He was joking. He's not good looking, not really, but he's a lovely man he makes you feel as if you're special. The ladies at Reception say he's been made student mentor so I picked the right person to go and see. I have a good instinct on picking people who can help me, Gray says it is spot on and I say, well I picked you didn't I?

So I told Gray that I'd missed the class accidentally but that I would make sure I didn't miss any more, and that Dr Gallagher had been really supportive and I didn't want to make things wrong between me and the uni. Gray just said that so long as I worked like I usually did because he hardly ever saw me he was sure that everything would be great. He's been great Gray, he didn't want to come and he was really cut up about leaving Tanya behind but as she was going to move out anyway sooner rather than later now she'd got her boyfriend Brian, it was time for us move on in our lives. We nearly had an argument. He said if we left the flat in Leeds he didn't know when we'd ever get another, but I said we didn't like Leeds. Did like the flat though he said, it was where Tanya was a baby and grew up. But I said she'd grown up now and he'd always gone on about leaving and going back to Newcastle. So leaving and coming here to something absolutely new to both of us was great, besides there's even less work in Newcastle for him, at least in a town where there's a uni there's more chance of me getting a job. It's not really a town he said, there's just one street and the rest is country, it's all flat and open. It's like out of a Western. You like Westerns I said. To watch he said, but I don't want to live in one. I do though I said I want to live in all sorts of stories. Anyway I said now he'd got the van we could go and walk up the mountains they weren't far from here or go on the lakes, bet you could hire boats or canoes, we could hire a canoe. He cheered up at the idea of a canoe, he loves the seaside. And the outdoors he's a real outdoors man bought a tent and everything when Tanya was little. So do I. We always go to Whitby every year, we would get there by train from Leeds, we didn't have a van in Leeds because he drove for the brewery though he borrowed one sometimes over a weekend off one of the drivers who were on the next site.

The week after I was earlier than her. It was hot and I had on a dress I made, Gray says the blue matches my eyes. She made some stupid remark about how she couldn't sew. I said why didn't you learn at school and she said it wasn't that kind of school. Too posh. Like her. Though how it was posh when it was half way across the world I didn't know. It was so hot and stuffy in the room I went to open the window and of course I wasn't able to and she made some clever clever comment about it being a special lock. To keep out undesirables. She said that was what Dr Farrington called them. Or it was her who said it and pretended it was Dr Farrington. Then she made me do another punctuation exercise, as if I was a school kid and it was going alright until I said where you punctuated was where the writer thought it was important that was what the lecturer in Leeds said. She ignored that and then I refused to do any more punctuation so she said what about learning to write an essay which I'd done in Leeds. And I told her the lecturer in Leeds he thought I wrote really well. She said it was different at university. I tried to explain to her that this wasn't really a proper class so I didn't have to do homework and that I didn't have time because I was working three nights at the pub and one day at the garden centre but she didn't take any notice. In the end she said to read a book and then write about it next time. She tried to choose the book for me as if she didn't think I could read either. Or knew anything.

I showed her because I wrote a great essay and she had to say it was great. I knew it was so I asked her to show it to Dr Young so he would see I could write an essay and Dr Gallagher. She asked why Dr Gallagher and I said well as she was going to be seeing him, seeing as he was her partner why not. She was shocked as if I'd been a nosy parker, but it served her right for telling Magda and Milosz all about me. Anyway I wasn't nosy, I just overheard the ladies in reception talk about her and him. How Dr Gallagher been here since he finished his Phd. How she'd not been here that long only about two years. How sad it was that his wife had gone back to America with his son. I felt really sorry for him, being left like that.

So I asked her for an extra class in our studio. Which I knew she wouldn't come, she wouldn't want to, but she couldn't say no so I went to their flat, to Dr Gallagher's I mean. I wanted to anyway. I wanted to see how he, how they lived. There were these white leather armchairs and a white leather settee. Really expensive, but I bet they weren't hers, I bet it was all there when she came. And there were books hers stacked on the floor and his papers stacked on the table. I couldn't live in such a scrow. I said so. And we talked about our schools hers foreign and different and mine just manky. It was scary up on our playground, there was fencing, but you looked right down into the street below, four storeys and one day one of the lads was dared to scramble up the fence, there was only a dinner lady on duty, and she didn't stop him, and he got right up to the top and half way over and the others shouted him on and he lost his balance. He was only ten. Then I looked at a photo of her mum and dad they didn't look friendly. And we talked about Dr Gallagher and Tom. I was hoping he would come back so I saw him in his home but it got later and later and she just sat there staring at me with those olive green eyes you can't see into because they're so dark and suddenly I was really scared. I knew she didn't want me there and I thought supposing she does something to me and I rushed to leave but she grabbed my hand and made me go down the stairs holding to it. It was horrible but I was able to keep my cool and before I went I asked about the garden, well it's only a square of green really with some bushes in the middle and a bird table that was on the other side of the block. She wouldn't have done anything to me, Gray said, he said it was the problem with my imagination and talent, sometimes my ideas went into overdrive. What I had to do was not let her get to me. So the next time I went to class which was after Gray and I had gone to the Appleby Fair and Gray had gone as brown as a berry, as brown as the gypsies I felt like them and all, being nomads, like them though Gray said he wasn't a nomad, he was a temporary resident in the west, and he preferred the north east, it didn't rain so much, it's hardly rained at all since we've been here, though it snowed once and my trainers got soaked, I made myself be very easy very business like, and quite friendly, caring Gray says I can be really business like when I want and I was like that for the rest of the course.

Brockenspectre

Ed

She thought I couldn't see her without my glasses – she'd tease me about how my thinking she was beautiful was literally a case of rosy-tinted spectacles – but I could. She was beautiful, but she didn't believe it. She said she was too tall, too thin, to be beautiful, but to me tall made her my equal. Laura was small and feminist. If she'd been a man she might have been accused of being a little man with a big stick, except she was funny in the peculiar fierce way of American humour. Very funny, but hard. Miriam wasn't funny. It was liberating. At least she was funny, sometimes, mostly because she was so vague.

With Laura I came to be on my guard at all times, waiting to be ambushed by a crack, which I wouldn't say was openly hostile, but had an element of hostility under the surface. Laura said it wasn't hostility, it was the truth, but it seemed antagonistic to me. We parted on reasonable terms, though logic says it was because she just packed up and went before we'd got to the stage of outright argument. She said she didn't want to live in Britain, she wanted to go home to the eastern seaboard. When I pointed out how impossible it would be for me to get work – proper work – in the States, as there were too many people and too few posts, and even getting a green card would take ages, she said I could be a house husband. Then Tom wouldn't have to go into an after school program. Try it for a year, she said. You know you love being there. You love the fall and the winter and the freedom of the long vacation. I didn't want to be a house husband. I've always worked. Even as a boy I had summer jobs. And there were too few posts in this country for me to risk giving up my job here. When I said this, she looked at me for a long time and then, in an unusually slow voice, said that she was being stifled by me and by the campus, and she wanted to bring up our son, her son, as an American with a 'can do' attitude. You, Ed, are cautious and conservative, she said, and I knew she was right. Not that Laura was wild, but nothing held her back from doing what she wanted. She knew her own mind. She went. She divorced me. I didn't contest it, and she got custody of Tom. I didn't contest the custody either. She wouldn't let him come to England for his holidays, in case he wanted to stay. That was her excuse. She meant in case I kept him here. So twice a year I've flown to the States. Sometimes for Christmas, sometimes for Tom's birthday, always in the long vacation.

Miriam was a relief. She listened to me, and although she was thin and lithe, where Laura was a little fat, her body was softer than Laura's, more willing to give to me than Laura's had ever been. The first week we were together at the conference it was an opening up. We walked the coast and talked about ourselves, and about how we were raised. Her upbringing seemed so different, so much freer than my slog to get out of Harlow. Much more privileged. We talked about Laura, how ambitious she was, not for herself – though with two degrees in maths she was able to get virtually any position she wanted in the American school system – but for Tom, opting to be a teacher in a private school in Massachusetts because she was then able to give him an education he could never get in a public school. I told her how his school was on the outskirts of a small town, and how Tom said the ripples of the river running past the buildings froze into waves in the winter.

We talked about her husband, Simon, and his affair,

which she wouldn't tell her children about because she didn't want to spoil him in their eyes. She was interested in my job, said how wonderful it was to talk to someone who believed in education for all, as she did. I told her of my love for the Lake District. I had come here for my interview via school in Essex and university in Wolverhampton, and never want to be separated from such beauty again. Not even the States, she asked? Not even the States, I said. Nowhere else had its self-sufficient, complete, loveliness. I knew she wouldn't criticise me, but I didn't tell her of my discussion with Laura, of my fear of leaving.

I knew with Miriam I would be happy, and persuaded her to come and visit me. Then, after she left Simon, she started coming up from Guildford, catching the last train on a Friday, going back first thing on the Monday, so we had the weekend to walk the fells.

One Saturday she picked up the staff vacancy list I'd brought. They're mostly administrative and domestic jobs, so we were both surprised to see a temporary post teaching language skills. I suggested she apply and said she could live with me.

I suppose I could, and write as well, she said. When I said you've kept that quiet, she said I've told you now, and I keep quiet about it because I'm not yet published. Do you think you will be, I asked. Yes, she said. For the first time I heard a quality in her voice which reminded me of Laura. Then she added, at least I hope I will. And she didn't remind me of Laura any longer.

She moved up just as the university commenced cutting back on academic staff, but language skills were always going to be needed for some of our students. The first year she had a class of thirteen, the year after two. Then I persuaded her to take on Hild. I got her money for the contact hours. She needed the work and Francesca needed Hild, she couldn't afford to lose another course from the campus. I told Miriam teaching Hild would maintain her connection with the university, and give her something to do in the summer. We were doubling up on roles and I no longer had the time to be with her.

I expanded on Hild manifesting herself like some kind of apparition, and the effect she had on us. Looking down at her like a bunch of dubious cows round a dog which has strayed into their field. Jeff's eyebrows going up and down because he wasn't sure about her and I knew what he was thinking. She laughed then, more freely than I ever heard her laugh before.

May

May is the month when everything begins.

It was the month when I cycled in the lanes around the campus, where the banks were full of violets and tiny white flowers Ed called eyebright. It was the month when I longed for my children most. I wanted them to be here, to feel the beauty with me. They left their universities and came. Not to the flat, but to camp on the western side of Windermere. I borrowed Ed's car and drove across to see them. They had the old tents from when they were young, and my sleeping bag with the mysterious black stain which appeared after one of their sleepovers. They had brought sausages and beer, porridge oats and milk, sugar and coffee. They begged me to stay the night.

I rang Ed, who was kind. He said of course you must.

They unleashed the canoe from the roof of my daughter's car, and launched it from a gravelly spit. They got in, almost turtling it, and shrieking, as they always did. I sat in the middle, my son at the back, my daughter at the front, and they paddled along the shore. A water lily stem was hooped above the lake. Its reflection rippled and flickered greenly, an electric eel. Up the Brathay, the weed, shredded silk, streamed in the river's flow. A heron stood, its neck cricked back, until the canoe was too close and it flapped heavily away.

'Look, its wings are outlined in blue.' My children were as delighted as I by its comedy and its indifference.

The following weekend the children were no longer here. I had a migraine. Ed and Jeff ran into you and Graham in the pub. Graham was proud of you, and you were solicitous for me.

At home, May was autumn and October was spring, but they weren't the same as spring and autumn here. The flowers blossomed and the leaves turned – at least they did where we lived – but there was not the feeling of change I encountered in England.

We knew winter was coming though, and with it the *Sudestada* which drove my mother insane. Almost literally insane. If it persisted for more than a day or two and was accompanied by the rain which streamed off the red tiled roofs, she became unpredictable. She would hide herself from the wind in her bedroom, emerging in the late evening to eat with my father, or, in between storms, she would go on excursions coming back with things she had acquired – a blue velvet dress for me, a rock and roll record for my father, things she thought we would like. And we did, but always with surprise. My father didn't listen to rock and roll – his taste in music was more sophisticated. I loved my blue velvet dress with its modesty insert of white taffeta – but it was too old for me. One day when it wasn't raining, she bought a dog. She borrowed my bike – I was the only one in the family to have one, my brother's holidays from school in England not long enough to warrant him a bike – and rode down to the stand of shops which were too far for me on my own, and bought it from the pet store there. She cycled back with the dog buttoned into her coat, its tiny beige head, the same colour as the coat, and triangle ears pricked above liquorice black eyes, peeking out from just underneath her collar. It was a Dobermann Pinscher she'd got for protection when my father was away on one of his business trips. It was an ugly little thing and my father christened it Feo.

The wind changed, my mother became sane and

handed the care of the pup to me. I fed him on boiled meat and dry biscuit, and when his fat round stomach was tickled, his little body squirmed, his stumpy tail beating out its pleasure. For he was a very little dog. Taking him for walks past villas with notices which said, "*Perro Peligroso*", Feo's size contrasted sharply with the Alsatians and Dobermanns who, with great clattering collisions, hurled themselves at the barred metal gates. One day, after I'd bought the *dulce de leche* which was fattening my thighs and plumping my breasts, we walked back past the garage. The mechanics' habitual wolf whistles died and they stooped to pat him. What variety of dog was it? He was a Dobermann, I said, and they snorted with laughter. He was they said, *claro qué sí*, not a German dog – not that they had anything against *los allemanos*, or, they added, *los ingléses* – but a South American dog, a Mexican Chihuahua.

I reported this conversation. My father said my mother had been sold a pup. My mother said she hadn't bought it – she had been given it because it was the runt of the litter. It became a running joke. Either way they were all wrong, my mother, my father, the mechanics, because Feo grew too big for a Chihuahua, but not big enough for a Dobermann. After the Christmas holidays he got a nasty attack of fleas and my father sent him up country to work as a cattle dog. The stupidity was that my mother was right. He was a Dobermann Pinscher, but a miniature, and by the time I found out, she was dead, and I wasn't able to tell her, and my father had gone to live in Chile.

May has too many possibilities. June is better. The weather is either good or bad, the hidden light gone. May is like October. There is danger in anticipation.

Picnic

I finished the last session I would ever have with you. You were elated. You'd graduated from the course and now nothing was standing in the way of your quest for a university education. Your thanks were effusive, but seemed sincere. You were not aware of how much you didn't know, but how could you – you had just embarked on the process.

I was filled with a sense of liberty, released back into my own life. Though it was mid-week, and there was work and school next day, some of the staff were driving off for an evening in the lakes, their cars primed with bikes, or towing sailing dinghies, or capped with kayaks. I watched the exodus, revelling in the summer. I could smell the heat. It reminded me of when I was small. Will and I had a shallow paddling pool set up under the apricot tree, the one which got covered every year in a black mat of caterpillars. The first year I was tall enough, when I was seven, I didn't know the caterpillars were there. I reached up to swing from the lowest branch and splash land into the pool below, and was stung from wrist to shoulder.

'Hi.' Ed had slipped in through the open front door to the flat without me hearing him.

'Ed.' I kissed him. 'Let's go out? Go over to Gowbarrow. You say it's an easy walk. And eat at a pub?' For an instant I had a vision of Ed and I lying in the long grass which I imagined covered the fell's flanks.

'Can we leave it until the weekend? I've quite a lot to do this evening.'

'Can't we be impulsive, Ed? We were once.'

'I've not been able to get to my emails.'

'Will it make any difference now?' I flopped over the back of the sofa and sprawled on the cushions.

'I'll be able to catch up.'

I lifted one leg, then the other into the air, regarding their length and my sandalled feet.

Ed looked down at me. His voice deepened, became husky. 'I got behind. Jeff and I had to see Francesca to okay his departmental outing Saturday week.'

'What's Jeff's outing got to do with you?'

Ed cleared his throat. 'The trip's popular, and the coach is full. He needs another vehicle. The Environmental Science minibus is the only one available.'

'So?'

'It's my department, Miriam. And I'm driving it. '

'Are you? Why? '

'After the literary rigours of Dove Cottage and Rydal Hall, Jeff wants to have a picnic near Rydal Cave – a "*dejeuner-sur-l'herbe*".'

I laughed. 'Do you think his students will appreciate a "*dejeuner-sur-l'herbe*"?

After a pause, while Ed stared down at me with what I was sure was longing, he continued. His attitude asked me to share his amusement.

'He needs the minibus to transport the picnic. And the Sherpas who are to carry it.'

'Sherpas? What are they? Who are they?'

'You know what they are, Miriam. I thought as the picnic is taking up Saturday we'd climb Loughrigg from Grasmere.'

'We?'

'Magda and Milosz. You.'

I was angry. 'You volunteered me?'

I got up. Ed moved towards me, but I put the table between us.

'I thought you'd like to – you keep saying you want more to do with the university.'

'Not as a *peón*. And I'm not sure I do, after Hild.'

I was halfway to the door.

'Where are you going?'

'Like I said. Out.'

'We'll go at the weekend, promise?' Was Ed pleading with me?

This time it was me who banged the entrance door so the glass rattled in its frame, but, unlike Ed, it wasn't a matter of habit. I went to the store to get my bike. Why hadn't I just said yes, gracefully, to acting as a *peón*? I'd had enough practice in the foothills of the Andes, where Will and I, in our children's ponchos, rode all day, the horses stopping dead as we leapt off and dropped our reins in search of tiny strawberries.

I'd refused because of you. Having taken you on I'd felt obliged to continue teaching you even when I didn't want to. I knew it was unjust to feel this, the things you told me – your defective education, your continual search for someone who would unlock your confidence, unlock you – revealed you as having been deprived, but they hemmed me in. It was particularly unjust because I had created the obligation which constrained me. I knew what it was to search for something or someone to unlock me. I knew yielding to the sensible – teaching you would stand me in good stead with the university – was the opposite of what I needed. It was a fetter I'd made for myself.

A week later, eight o'clock in the morning found me waiting for the coach and the minibus along with Jeff and his students. There were the usual alarms. One student phoned to say she was running late, and another, a friend of Milosz from Manchester, Chris – how he'd got on the trip I didn't know – had to race to the newsagents to buy tobacco and cigarette papers. Nicole arrived from Carlisle. I hadn't seen her since early January – she'd kept away from the Founder's Day lecture. She was wearing a floppy hat with a large green rose pinned to it. Jeff had invited her as official photographer of the *dejeuner-sur-l'herbe,* but she was travelling with the Sherpas. She seemed to find the term comic. Jeff, she informed me with delight, had used Sherpa wrongly. A Sherpa was a guide not a porter. Not even a guide, a tribe. She made me smile, and the students posed, more than willing to have their photographs taken by her.

Jeff loomed over me, 'Thanks for helping, Miriam.'

'There's no need to thank me.'

'But there is. You and Magda and Milosz are carrying the picnic. I feel duly grateful.'

Was he being sarcastic?

The coach ground up the drive, reversed, and parked facing down it. It was followed by the minibus with Ed at the wheel. You were sitting beside him.

Jeff was surprised, 'I didn't know Hild was coming.'

So was I. 'Was she asked?'

'Yes, I thought as she was already *in situ* she might as well join in. But she said she wanted to spend the day with her husband, what's he called? '

'Graham. Gray. She must have changed her mind.'

Ed backed around the shrubs. Your hands fluttering, you were talking volubly. You leant across Ed.

'Isn't it a beautiful morning? Ed found me at the car park. I thought I might miss you.'

'Wonderful, but hot for walking uphill,' Nicole called

back. She turned to me, 'Who's that?'

'Hild Whittaker, I've been tutoring her.'

'This is the first time Hild's been on a fell. It's a good one to begin with. There's a lot to see from a very small height,' Ed said.

He got out and opened the rear door so we could load up. Magda and Milosz threw their rucksacks in on top of Ed's. Nicole and I squeezed ours next to a day pack which I assumed belonged to you. Then we clambered into the bus.

Nicole started to say something, but I cut in, 'I thought you and Graham had done the walk from Pooley Bridge to Hallin Fell– '

'It was in Gray's van.'

'But– '

'Or was it the other place . . . where the waterfall is.'

'Aira Force?' Nicole offered.

You fell in with her suggestion and nodded.

Over his shoulder Ed sent me a look which implied I wasn't being tactful. 'Maybe you misunderstood what Hild said, Miriam?'

The coach set off and we followed behind. I half listened to your conversation with Nicole – you loved the town, it had everything you needed, you loved the country, Graham was much happier here than in Leeds even though you had to leave your seventeen-year-old daughter behind with her boyfriend's family.

Ed was wrong. It wasn't the sort of thing I misunderstood. Besides, I remembered it clearly. It came up in the first class after you had visited the flat. You'd been to Appleby Fair, sleeping in Graham's bakery van, and were beguiled by your affinity with the travellers. You'd returned the next day via the top end of Ullswater – and Hallin Fell.

The coach stopped at Dove Cottage and half of

Jeff's group got out. We stopped also, so Ed and Jeff could make sure of their timings. The coach carried on to Rydal and Ed drove the minibus to the car park on the outskirts of Grasmere.

We had four hours to get to the rendezvous at the cave. If you were young, as Milosz and Magda were, or fit, as Ed, Nicole and me were, it wasn't a demanding route. I wasn't sure about you, though you showed us a new pair of boots with exuberance.

'Aren't they great, Miriam?'

'Have you broken them in, Hild?'

You were blithe. 'Well if they get uncomfortable, I can always– '

'I have plasters in my first aid,' Nicole interrupted, 'but I bet you were going to say, "Take them off".' She smiled sympathetically and your laughter bubbled up.

Ed and I had done this walk several times, yet I could never remember the way to its start. I always thought we came into the village from the other end, and it always caught me out when we reached the wall around the church.

At the lychgate, Ed said, 'Anyone want to go and look at Wordsworth's grave?'

'Who is Word-es-worth?' Milosz asked.

'One of our great poets, Milosz, he came from round here,' you said. 'I expect Miriam's seen it before, but I haven't. I'd like to. Do you want to, Milosz? Magda?

Milosz gave the tiniest shrug. The burial place of a dead English poet was of no more interest to him than creative writing, but Magda agreed to go with you.

'It's opposite the east end of the church.' Ed said, as he pointed them in the right direction.

Nicole and Milosz propped themselves against the wall. I laid my hand on it. It was cool and damp from the night air.

'I am going to get a hit of my favourite spice. Jeff's commissioned me to pick up gingerbread. You coming in, Miriam?'

The shop was too tiny to accommodate anything other than two bodies. Ed and I took off our rucksacks. As we emerged, the handles of the carrier bags straining under the weight of all the packets, you and Magda returned.

'I've taken a picture.' You brandished your mobile phone at us.

'Well done,' Ed said. He went on, 'The gingerbread needs to be divided between us, there's too much for one or two people.'

'It should go at the bottom.' Nicole was, as always, practical.

'We're not unpacking everything now, Nicole,' Ed was firm.

'It'll squash the rest of the food.' Nicole was equally firm.

'Jeff should have thought of it before he decided on a literary dessert,' Ed replied.

'I can take some,' you said eagerly.

'That's all right, Hild, I don't suppose you're used to walking up hills. I can carry both gingerbread and my camera this year. You can carry it for me next.'

'Does this happen every year?'

'Every year, like the Founder's Day lecture. And a number of other events.'

Nicole's wry comments about the university made me wonder why she wasn't freelance. With her reputation and earning power she didn't need to be Senior Lecturer in the Creative Arts Department.

'Next year. I'll be almost a second-year student – it'll

be great.'

The double 'l' in both I'll and it'll was intensified. You sounded as you had when you first came to class. Since that time you'd veered between hostility and a kind of febrile excitement with me. Recently you'd displayed an indifferent politeness.

Ed was indulgent of your see-saw emotions. Or rather he rationalised them. He said he thought such swings showed your lack of self-esteem, which would disappear as you gained in academic confidence. I had my doubts. Your volatility seemed to come from something more than lack of self-esteem, and I thought he placed too much faith in education.

The road was crowded with walkers, mostly tourists out for a half-day stroll which gave excellent views, and families who didn't want to have to drag their children too far. They meandered along in T-shirts and shorts, water bottles in hand. Even at ten-thirty it was hot. Cars came down Red Bank and met the cars crawling up from the village. To allow them to pass we fell into single file, and, from time to time, we had to halt.

Pressing herself against a wall, Nicole said dryly, 'Next year, recommend to Jeff he chooses a week day for his arty-outing, Ed.'

As we set off you tied yourself to Ed's heels, but now you dropped back to where I was acting as sweeper. Sweat stippled your forehead and greased the curve of your nostrils. The crevice between your breasts was shiny. You were going pink. I was sweating, but my breasts don't have a cleft between them. I twisted my hair into a knot, fastened it and turned up the collar of my shirt to stop my neck getting burnt.

'It's really hot.'

'Not much further to some shade.' I looked at your shoulders. 'Have you anything else to wear, Hild? Have you sunscreen?'

'No.'

'Ed's got some. You must put it on when you get to the woods.'

'I didn't think it would be so hot.'

Ten minutes later we entered the woods. The others were already gathered on one side of the path, Magda and Milosz, fingers linked, leaning against a tree. Nicole and Ed had taken off their rucksacks. Ed maintained it maximised the rest, but I was never sure it was worth the effort.

'Drinks,' said Ed.

'Anyone got a spare shirt they can lend Hild?'

No one had.

'Have you the sunscreen, Ed?'

He rummaged through the outside pockets of his rucksack and handed the tube to me. I squirted it onto your back and your neck, and, rubbing the cream over your plump shoulders, restrained a sudden vindictive urge to squeeze them hard. I handed the tube to you so you could do your arms and chest.

Nicole regarded your flushed face with concern. 'I don't really need my hat. You can borrow it if you want. The straw's a bit broken, but it'll shade the most delicate bits.'

The hat was too large for you, and hid you from view, but you greeted it with cries of joy and put it on, the green rose flopping limply on the brim as you thanked her. Ed bit his lip and stole a look at Milosz, who remained impassive, though Magda smiled.

Helped by an unexpected breeze which had found its way off Grasmere, everyone speeded up. Milosz and Magda moved off with Nicole. You recovered your bounce and your position at Ed's side, directing a stream of talk at him. Left on my own I enjoyed the peace, entertained by the knowledge Ed, trapped by his role, wasn't able to shut you up.

I came out of the trees for the climb to Loughrigg and found you waiting for me. You had slipped down the line, left behind by Ed's efficient stride, overtaken by Nicole, whose legs climbed the steps of the path as if they were her stairs at home. Milosz and Magda were way ahead. I was faster than you, but, remembering the rule to never leave the slowest member of the group on their own, I matched my pace to yours.

'Aren't they great?' you asked, panting a little. You took off your pack, took out an inhaler, and puffed it twice into your mouth. Ed had to know you had asthma. Surely.

'I bet you wish you could walk like them, without stopping, Miriam.'

'I can, and they do – to look at the view.'

'They do? I'll catch up with Ed and the rest?'

The pungent scent of the bracken lost its usual, baffling enticement. Your question was hungry. It seemed you possessed several varieties of greed. Or the same greed but for different objects.

'Yes – but as soon as you reach them they'll be off and leave you to enjoy it on your own. The one thing this group doesn't do together is look at the view. Until they reach the top.'

Your dejection pleased me.

Always a slog, the stone ladder with you was interminable, some of the steps very nearly too high for you. In the full sun it was sweltering. Your grovel and apology for holding me back made me wonder if you were also greedy for unkindness, but beneath your blaming yourself I thought you were cross. I might be keeping you company, but you gave me the same feeling I'd had in the flat. Then, I was uncertain what you wanted or who you wanted. Persuaded you wanted one of us, today you didn't want me, and I resented Ed going ahead and leaving you with me.

When we got to the summit I let you plod in front. Your gait was leaden. You had taken off Nicole's hat to fan yourself, and your soaked hair was the colour of pewter.

'Thanks for waiting,' I said.

Ed's glasses flashed in my direction.

'No, I mean it. I can't identify the fells as you can. Hild wants to know what they are.'

Ed waved his arm, 'Take a look around, Hild, there's not a better sight in the Lake District from such a low level.'

'Except perhaps from Hallin Fell?'

Ed's glasses flashed at me again. It was the third warning he had given me and it didn't lessen my resentment.

'Sorry, I forgot. You didn't hike there, did you, Hild?'

Nicole, the diplomat, took you by the elbow and led you to the old trig point.

'From here you can see . . .' Nicole began naming the peaks '. . . Dollywaggon, Great Rigg, Fairfield, Heron Pike . . .' She had walked and photographed all of them. Sweeping the fells with his binoculars, Ed followed the litany while Milosz raised his shoulders in faintly bored enquiry at Magda. She jerked her head in the direction of Rydal Water, 'We go to the cave,' and they moved away.

Ed lowered his binoculars.

'You're being unfair, Miriam.'

Was I? My annoyance deepened to mutiny. I raised my eyebrows and didn't reply.

Ed's lips straightened.

'We'll meet you at the cave, Nicole,' he called. She flapped her hand in acknowledgement without turning round.

'Are you leaving Nicole on her own with Hild?'

'Why not? Loughrigg isn't Helvellyn.'

He set off down the path. I realised Magda and Milosz weren't in sight.

'Is this the right path for the cave? I don't think Magda and Milosz came this way, it might take us longer.'

'No, it won't, the paths will join up in a minute.'

I scrambled down after him to the boggy bit at the bottom. Usually I had to hop from tussock to tussock, Ed deriding me lightly when I missed one and my boots filled up with water. Now it was dry and Ed ignored me.

Thunderclouds were building over Morecambe Bay.

'How long before the storm hits us?'

'It'll be several hours. Don't fret, Miriam.'

'I'm not fretting.'

Midges hung low, close above my head. According to Ed, their height indicates atmospheric pressure. Noting the speed with which the clouds filled the horizon, I wondered if the storm was hours off. To me the Sherpas looked to be drenched on the walk back to Grasmere.

Without speaking, Ed veered onto a track gashed across the hause. I had been publicly unpleasant to Hild, and by extension rude to Nicole, Magda and Milosz. He was cross, and in a hurry to reach the rest of the party.

I didn't remember the track, but then I always found Loughrigg queer, difficult to fix in my mind. I started to look for the lone holly tree which was for me the signpost to the cave. Instead, we reached a wall, the ground beneath it rutted and uneven where it had been pounded by boots in the winter. Another five minutes and there was a wood, which puzzled me, as I didn't recall either a wall or a wood until the drop down to the lake. The wood on my right disappeared and another track through yet another copse emerged on my left. Then we joined a road.

For two or three minutes I marched along behind Ed, who was drawing away from me fast, before calling after him, 'Ed, let's look at the map.'

He called back, 'Why, Miriam?'

'Because I don't recognise where I am.'

He stopped and walked towards me. 'All right. Get it out.'

'I didn't bring one. I thought you had.'

'I don't bother on Loughrigg – not unless there's going to be low cloud or mist. And you always carry one.'

'I thought you said it was a very muddling fell – brilliant for a map reading exercise, you said, when you first brought me here.'

'It is muddling, and brilliant – but only in foul weather.'

'Do you remember a road on the way to the cave?'I insisted.

'No.'

'Well.'

'Well what?'

'The weather isn't bad and Loughrigg is still muddling.'

Ed frowned at me. He knew I was right. He got out his Sigg bottle, took a swallow, wiped the top and handed it to me.

I refused.

'You ought to drink.'

'I don't want any.' I wasn't making peace with a mouthful of lukewarm water.

He stowed the bottle in silence.'We need to get on.'

'Would it be better to go back to where we went wrong?'

'To the top of Loughrigg? We're late already.'

'Would we have to go to the top?'

Ed looked up and down the road. 'Which direction does the road run?'

'How should I know?' I knew I was jeopardising something other than what should have been a pleasurable trip.

He made no move to take his compass out and I realised he hadn't brought a compass either. Nor had I.

Ed lifted his wrist and aimed his watch at the sun.

'There's south, so that's north.'

'Yes.'

'Don't just say "yes", Miriam.'

I looked down. Was that my shadow, or was it a darker patch of tarmac?

'I think south is that way and my shadow is pointing north.'

'So west is where the wall runs. It must go up and over Lanty Scar.'

'A scar?'

'It shouldn't be too bad, it's not very high.'

I didn't mind boulders and high steps, but I hated clambering down rock faces. I heaved my rucksack, saturated with my sweat, onto my shoulders. I knew what Ed was thinking – Lanty Scar would be the quickest and we mustn't be any later than we already were. Nicole, Magda, Milosz and I had the inessentials: the salad, the fruit and the gingerbread. Ed had the basics, the sandwiches.

As Ed and I came into sight, the students yelled, 'There's Dr. Gallagher.'

'Hey, Dr Gallagher, where's lunch? The 'erbe's 'ere but the dejeuner ain't.' Chris's inversion of the phrase earned him a covert glance from Ed, who, however, managed to raise a grin.

'Hold on. Lunch is being delivered to you right now.'

'What happened?' Jeff was too relieved to be accusing.

'How's the literary picnic? Were you worried?'

I knew Ed's unconcern was assumed, annoyed with himself as he was for getting lost, but it was provocative and I had sympathy for Jeff.

'I was. The literary picnic will be more satisfying when we've had the main course.'

'We've eaten such gingerbread, fruit and salad as we had. In that order.' Nicole's humour had acquired a slight edge.

'They're rather boisterous.' Ed surveyed the picnickers over his glasses, his way of not having to see them.

'There's been quite a lot to drink. And a variety of games in the furze. I've some excellent photos.' Nicole smiled to herself with a private amusement.

Jeff, ill at ease, was terse. 'Dish the food out, Ed.'

'Sorry.'

Ed skimmed packets of sandwiches at the students. 'Will they do?'

They fell upon them, tearing them open, and with derisive hoots of, "egg salad", "ham", "cheese savoury", rammed the food into their mouths.

'And now, hopefully, they will not suffer alcohol poisoning. However, as I'm merely a Sherpa,' Nicole inspected her sandwich for its filling, 'it's not my problem.'

When Ed and I arrived you had been sitting with Magda, Milosz and Chris. You half got up, but Ed and Jeff turned to look out over the ravine which plunged down to Rydal, mumbling to each other as they too rammed their mouths, and you sat back down.

I slumped beside Nicole. My legs were trembling with the climb down Lanty Scar and the effort to keep up with Ed.

'Egg salad? Ham? Cheese savoury?' She repeated the students' chorus. 'Not an exceptionally imaginative choice for a *dejeuner-sur-l'herbe*, but filling.'

'No, thanks, I'll have a drink. Racing along behind Ed killed my appetite.'

Nicole passed me some lemonade.

'Did it?' Her question was casual, but I could tell she thought my lack of hunger an unusual reaction to comparatively easy walking, whatever the speed.

'Came over Lanty Scar.'

'You did? It's out of your way – can be nasty too. How interesting. Forgot the map co-ordinates? Miss the turning?' She was being sardonic – she knew Ed was too good a fell walker to do either of these things.

'Missed the turning off the hause. No map or compass.'

She contemplated me. 'Have some gingerbread.'

As I broke the slab along its groove, Jeff said, 'I reckon we're in for a storm.'

Ed and I had been so intent on getting to the picnic I'd forgotten about the weather. I looked up. Jeff was right. The clouds had turned the colour of dried mustard. Then a thunderbolt cracked on the summit and there was a huge crash. The storm was on top of us.

'Leave your gear. Get into the cave.'

Clasping bottles and cans, the students obeyed, bounding along the rocky path, followed in the rear by Nicole, Milosz and Magda. Chris stooped for the last of the gingerbread before he sprinted after them. I ran, Ed and Jeff behind me. Where the path turned I looked back. In the half-light the rucksacks were like coloured sheep bedded down before the rain to come. Gusts of wind lifted polystyrene containers which skipped and fell as if they were alive. You stood in the middle of this debris with your arms wrapped over your head.

'Ed, Jeff. Hild.'

They raced towards you, wrenched your hands down, took you by the upper arms, lifted you off your feet, and hustled you into the middle of the cave. Chris, Magda, Milosz and I stayed near the entrance. The rest of the students disposed themselves where they could, along with other walkers who had been similarly caught out.

The cave erupted. The boom of the thunder and your shrieks fused and repeated, echoing back inside the low roof. Nicole's camera exploded, criss-crossing the lightning again and again, until we were blinded. At every burst you screamed, trembled, tried to cover your eyes, but Ed and Jeff held onto you and your hands weren't able to reach your face. The noise was engulfing and isolating. Outside, rain steamed and churned from the trees beneath us. Hail clattered, the temperature plummeted. In the murk of the cave your tremble became a shudder.

When the lightning thinned and the thunder had rumbled into the distance, we left the cave. Nicole emerged with her camera in her hand, examining the photos she had taken at the same time as watching where she placed her feet, with the occasional speculative look at you as you stumbled out, your arms clasped by Jeff and Ed, your body limp, your face blank.

Jeff decided you were in no fit state to walk the two miles to Grasmere. Besides, it was still raining and he discovered you had no waterproof. Nicole, who had evidently had enough of this outing, said she thought you deserved the support of a female member of staff. When Jeff objected that there weren't enough seats in the coach for Nicole as well, she was direct. He would have to give up his seat and sit on the steps by the driver. Someone else would take Hild's, your, place in the minibus. In this mood Nicole was daunting. Jeff yielded, and Chris, not being one of his students, volunteered to walk back to Grasmere with his friends Magda and Milosz.

What Milosz and Magda thought of all this I didn't know, but while Chris scavenged the tinfoil which glinted wetly on the fell, they worked without complaint, rescuing the polystyrene from the impromptu streams now flowing down its side. This was a student excursion they wouldn't forget, but they were too diplomatic to comment.

Going back along Loughrigg Terrace, they walked three abreast in front of me and Ed. Chris began to sing, "We've tried it once, we've tried it twice and found it rather nice". The second time through, Milosz and Magda joined in.

At the third rendition Magda asked me, 'What does "Roall me oaver in the cloaver" mean?'

Milosz pushed her into the now glistening bracken, saying, 'I will show you. Ha,' so I didn't have to answer.

Ed said nothing, either then, or on the drive back. The three of them engrossed in a discussion of the merits and demerits of English and European folk music – it emerged that Chris was a musician – didn't notice. At least, I didn't see any sideways looks. Ed left them outside Magda and Milosz's flat on the high street, left me at the main gate and went to park the minibus behind the technical building.

The storm hadn't refreshed the air, thunder muttered away in the fells, and the temperature was rising. Normally I loved heat enwrapping me, it made my world right, but Ed's silence was solid, and my world was wrong.

My muscles stretched from climbing over Lanty Scar, chilled from the cave and damp from the rain, I ran a very hot bath, lay back in the water and wished this was the good end to a day's walking. But I knew it wasn't the end, it was an interlude. The standoff between me and Ed was still to be resolved.

I heard him come in. He went into the kitchen and his Sigg bottle clinked sharply on the counter. He threw his boots into the hall cupboard. They hit the vacuum cleaner and knocked over the broom. He swore. Had the broom hit him, or had he sworn because of mounting irritation? There was the glug of liquid poured into a glass. The fridge or freezer door opened. Ice cubes cracked out of their tray. Freezer. They were thrown into the glass. He was drinking whisky. Neat.

I let the water out of the bath, tucked my towel around me and went through to the bedroom to get dressed. Ed sat in his armchair, his back to me, and didn't bother to turn around. He had the television on and was watching baseball live from the States. Usually he only watched a game after he'd had a conversation with Tom and was reminded of the real distance between them.

I put on a skirt and a T-shirt. I wanted to obliterate the day, and you, and me. I crossed to the kitchen, poured myself a whisky, added melting ice cubes, went back to the living room and sat on the sofa. Ed glowered at the television. The early dark which followed the storm gathered in the window behind me. I finished my drink. I got up and went to the kitchen.

'What are you doing?'

'Getting myself another scotch.'

'Is that wise?'

'Probably not.'

'You know you can't drink scotch, Miriam.'

'I know.'

'You'll have a migraine.'

'If I do, I'll deal with it. I can sleep tomorrow.'

I returned with my new drink. From earlier instruction I could see the batter had stayed put at the plate the whole time. All the balls had pitched foul.

Ed got up and poured himself more whisky.

He came back in. 'You shouldn't have done it.'

I thought I understood what he meant, but I wasn't prepared to help him. 'Done what?'

'When Hild said she and Gray went to Hallin Fell, you insinuated she was lying. You shouldn't have.'

'Is it such a sin?'

'It is when it is in public.'

'Why?'

I knew the answer before I asked the question. Insinuating someone is lying in public is a sin against propriety. Even worse, in Ed's view, it was a sin against the impartiality of an educator.

'Because you embarrassed her?' He was not friendly.

'Is that a rhetorical question?'

'For goodness sake.'

'Did I embarrass her?'

My question was not rhetorical. I didn't think you were embarrassed.

'Of course you did.'

'Well why did she tell me she and Graham had gone up there if it wasn't true? And does anyone care if she did?'

'She cares, she wants to– '

'She wants to what?'

Ed restrained himself. 'Become something she isn't

– yet.'

'So she lied to me about having gone fell walking and tells you the truth?'

'When she talks with you, Miriam, she tries to make herself more like you – '

'I don't get it. How do you know she wasn't lying to you and not to me?'

'It doesn't matter whether it's you or me she lies to, Miriam – if she does. Maybe they're all half truths. You can't actually go up Hallin Fell by van – you know you've got to get out and walk the last bit.'

'To become something she isn't yet, she tells lies to one or other of us, and it doesn't matter to you whether she has or hasn't. In which case why are you worried?'

'Several times you've appeared to doubt her, her . . .' Unable to identify my attitude, he trailed off, but his suspicion coming on top of his anger infuriated me.

'Her honesty? I've not queried her. Until today. She was the one who told me she had walked up Hallin Fell.'

'Had been up Hallin Fell – anyway it's not a real fell. It's the motorists' fell.'

I glared at him. 'In my innocence I repeated it . . . and now I am being blamed for it? '

'Don't shout, Miriam.'

I spoke even louder. 'Why not?'

'Because you know how thin the walls are.'

'We're sitting on the far side of the stairwell in the middle of this building, and you tell me not to shout.'

'And you can probably be heard in The Close– '

'Don't be ridiculous.'

Ed's expression said "be ridiculous" amounted to saying he was ridiculous. Now, as well as disturbing everyone, and by implication, spoiling the picnic, I had insulted him. I had shown myself to be emotional, but not in the class of emotion Ed liked.

'You think what I said about Hallin Fell was deliberate.'

'No.'

'Yes, you do.'

Ed turned to face me. 'All right, I thought you probably did say it on purpose, you've had a down on her ever since . . .' He didn't finish.

'Ever since she persuaded you and Jeff Young and Francesca Farrington that what she wanted – what she wanted – was in the interest of the university. I don't know of any other student who could achieve it. And no, I don't have a down on her. How dare you think that? I've been trying to help.'

'But Miriam, you were willing to give your time–'

'And I get blamed for being nasty. To someone I am trying to help. And I haven't. Been nasty.'

'Then why did you make the comment when you reached us.'

'Because I was left to escort Hild, and she would have rather have accompanied the rest of you. Especially you.'

'How can you possibly tell she wanted to be with me?'

'You can always tell. She didn't welcome my company. She lost her animation. She was dissatisfied.'

As I said this I realised I didn't know if not feeling welcome, apart, perhaps, from his break up with Laura, was something Ed had ever experienced.

'Maybe she found the going hard. I don't think she's entirely fit.'

'Maybe you, as the leader, should have thought about her fitness before you let her come. She used an inhaler today.'

'How could I say no?' He said nothing for a bit.

Then. 'I think you should apologise to Hild.'

'What?'

'A sort of "hope she's okay after today's ordeal", apology.'

'Really?'

Again Ed said nothing. We'd had quarrels before, but this was the first real row, full of hate.

'Go and see Hild tomorrow?'

'Why?'

'Because she's a student.'

He didn't look at me. He took his glasses off and polished them, which told me he was very unhappy – or very angry. Certainly not changing his mind.

'Only if you come too.' Each word was a struggle, sticking to my tongue.

Ed got up and came over to me. He touched my hand. He hoped the argument was over. 'Cook a pizza, watch the baseball?'

'I'll go and see her but I won't apologise. You'll have to do that.'

If I conciliated you, like I did over your essay, where would it lead?

I had another drink despite the loom of a migraine. Sometime later Ed carried me to bed. I don't remember if we made love.

I had a migraine of a ferocity which reminded me of my history lessons, of Cardinal Mazarin, whose migraines were so bad, the pain so intense, he shut himself into his room and whinnied like a horse.

From the perfunctory quality of his sympathy I understood Ed felt I had let him down, but nothing would get me out of bed. To the pillow which covered my head he announced he would go and see if you and Graham were in.

'To say what?

'Like I said last night. To say I hope she wasn't distressed by the way her first time on the fells worked out – the storm and everything.'

'Don't mention me.'

'If I have to.'

'Why should you have to?'

'Don't talk, Miriam, it'll make you feel worse.'

I slept.

I was on an ancient train rattling over the rails. It was getting dark and I was travelling diagonally through Europe to England. From Hungary? I was trying to escape. At my feet, covered with a rug, there was a large food basket. The conductor and the guard came in and asked for my ticket. I handed it to them. The risk was very great. The basket contained the baby I was rescuing. They slid the door closed with a bang.

I woke up, my heart racing, the dream torn from me. The bang was the front door to the flat. Ed was at my side, smiling and happy. Despite the danger, I wanted my dream back.

'How are you?'

'Much the same.'

'You've slept. Do you need anything: tea, coffee, juice?'

'Glass of water.'

He brought me a pint glass, and dropped an envelope onto the bed.

'A note from Hild.'

'I'll read it later.'

'Read it now, it might cheer you up.'

I tore scraps of paper from the back of the envelope until Ed took it away from me and opened it. He handed me a card. I screwed my eyes up because the light was dim and my head was being stilettoed, as though I still had the knife a boyfriend once gave me and was attacking my own skull with it. Your handwriting was even tinier than usual.

"Dear Miriam, So sorry to hear you that you have a migraine, they must be horrid, I've never had one myself. I thought you were looking a bit pale yesterday, when everyone else was either red or brown what causes them? Perhaps it was all that walking, and the excitement of the thunderstorm, and you and Ed getting lost because you didn't take any maps with you. Nicole said about that, she was lovely to me on the way back, saying what a star I was for walking so well on my first time in the Lake District proper, just a shame I am so frightened of thunderstorms, I hate anything sudden and loud noises like fights and things. You are a wonderful lady, putting up with all that when it isn't even your job, I am learning from you how to put up and shut up. With best wishes from Hild and Gray sends his too."

I handed the card to Ed who scanned it.

'She doesn't appear to be bearing a grudge. Maybe the episode has sorted things out and when university starts back it will be a new beginning.'

I was in too much pain to comment. I closed my eyes and after a couple of seconds Ed laid a warm hand on my forehead and said he and Jeff were going gill scrambling.

It was important to know if I saved the child, and I tried to re-enter my dream, but it had gone.

'We've had our wrists slapped. By Francesca.'

Ed sounded cross. He put a memo slip on my lap top. One of the kind Francesca used to communicate with her senior staff when an email wouldn't do.

I brushed it off the keys. I loved Ed, lived with him, but I wasn't having him touch my computer. He was invading my work.

'And she's not happy about the incident between you and Hild.'

'What incident?'

'Your . . . your accusation.'

'How does Francesca know?'

'Things get about.' Ed was offhand.

'If people talk. Only if people talk. There were six of us on top of Loughrigg.'

'What does it matter how she found out? You must be more careful, Miriam.'

'I get on well with Milosz and Magda. And Nicole. I'll bet Hild said something to Jeff, which he's repeated to Francesca. Shit. Or rather what a shit.'

'Miriam, you don't know, I don't know how it got about. It's irrational to go blaming Jeff– '

I threw the memo at him. It flapped to the floor like detritus from an incinerator.

I knew it was irrational, but your coming here had divided me and Ed on at least two occasions now, and it frightened me. It made me wonder who Ed was and what I was doing here.

Hild

The picnic was great. Well most of it was. It would have been greater if she hadn't been there. I wasn't expecting her to be. Dr Young said as I had been in classes with her I was eligible to go on the English department picnic but he didn't say she was going to be there, though he said Dr Gallagher, Ed, was driving the mini-bus. He called it a dejeuner sur herbe which is some kind of a gag about a picture. Nicole explained it to me. I said I wasn't sure as it was Saturday and Gray and I usually went somewhere, Carlisle or Preston or Ambleside because although Gray gets on with people he is quite shy and a bit lonely. He's never been really matey. When he had his own car it was second hand in Durham he used to spend hours doing it up. But then he lost his job and had to sell it. That's when he came down to Leeds and we got married and I was working behind the bar at the cricket ground. Anyway when I woke up on the Saturday I said to Gray would he mind if I went because it would only be the once and we could go somewhere nice the next Saturday. And he said of course he didn't mind and I said I'd make it up to him and I put on my new boots which I bought specially and rushed off to the car park where the science minibus was parked and I got there just in time as Dr Gallagher, Ed, was driving off to the meeting place up at the Old House. It was a beautiful day the sky was blue, the same blue as my eyes. I know because Gray told me as I was leaving our flat.

The coach was already there and there was lots of young students standing around. And her. I didn't expect her to be there because she's told me she doesn't really like being with large groups of people. What she likes is being on her own. And Magda and Milosz and a woman with a camera, that was Nicole, and Dr Young, and her. She introduced me to Nicole and I said jokingly, aren't my new boots great and she said, that's Miriam said, were they broken in or something stupid like that and Nicole said she had a first aid kit if I got blisters. Us six were in the mini bus not the big coach because we were going to be sherpas, that was another gag, I think it was Dr Gallaghers, Eds, or it might have been Dr Youngs, and carry the picnic, but I didn't mind because I was with people I knew and liked and who liked me. Apart from her. She's not very friendly. The photo of her mum and dad wasn't friendly either. It was as if they were made different by being abroad. Because it is a bit scary being with loads of people who don't know you. I sat beside Dr Gallagher and he said to call him Ed, which I did anyway in my mind, and I have done with her, and that's when it started. He said it was my first time on the fells and she said it wasn't. He seemed a bit put out and said she must have made a mistake so I changed the subject and talked about how wonderful Gray and I felt it was to be in such a cosy little town, it had all we needed really. And it was such a lovely campus. Being there was more like being in a film than at uni, like the big houses in Four weddings and a Funeral with the Old House with its pillars and the admin building looking like a glass sail against the sky. Ed said it was a good description of the admin block. And I said the sports hall was great, not that I played sport. And all the trees around the lawn in front of the Old House. I made them laugh when I said about Gray thinking it was like the wild west, one street and all around flat except for the little slope up to Old House. Nicole said if Gray wanted the wild west he'd only to go to Carlisle or Barrow on a weekend.

When we got to Grasmere I went to see the

Wordsworth grave and took a picture and she didn't even answer when I said had she seen it but Magda came with me. After we came back and they'd got the gingerbread we started walking. I was in front with Ed. We walked past a garden centre and a hotel and then past a sweet little tea house on the edge of the small lake, and it was so hot. I didn't expect it to be that hot and I hadn't got any water and my shoulders started burning. And we had to keep stopping because there was loads of people and cars and it was so hot and the pollen or the car exhaust made me pant so I couldn't keep up with Ed and the others and I had to walk with her. She looked at my shoulders and said have you got anything to cover them with? I wanted to say what's it to you, but I didn't because I didn't want to fall out with her. She seemed so cross with me. All I was trying to do was become part of the uni. It's as if she didn't want me to get on. It's all right for her, she's got her degree, two she said, one in languages and translating, Spanish and French I think, as well as one for teaching English. She's got everything she wants. As we got under the trees it was better she rubbed some sunscreen on my shoulders and Nicole lent me her hat, it was so large it covered me up, and I got to talk to Ed. I was telling him about Tanya and about my lectures in Leeds, he was very interested. But when we came out of the woods Ed and the others all went so fast up these huge steps up the hill I couldn't keep up and I had to walk with her again.

When we got to the top I was running with sweat, though she wasn't, she looked quite cool. And then she started on how I wanted to know about the names of the mountains and she couldn't tell me because she didn't know because she was a stranger too and how it was my first time up a fell except one. And Ed looked, well he didn't look anything. He looked as if he might be cross, because it wasn't fair that she was going on about it me saying I had been up Hallin Fell, when I hadn't not really. So Nicole she told me to put the hat back on I'd taken it off because my head was so hot, and then showed me the fells. Ed said he was going to the rendezvous at the cave and Nicole said see you there. It was a beautiful walk down the side of the mountain and Nicole showed me a little flower called the speedwell which she said was the colour of my eyes and we chewed some berries that she said were used to make gin.

The others from the coach had arrived by the time we got to the picnic and they were all drinking beer and stuff. I sat with Magda and Milosz and someone called Chris who kept smoking rollies and it was blowing my way so I asked him to move around the other side of me because it makes my breathing worse. After a bit when Ed and her hadn't come the students were getting really drunk and started jumping on each other in the bracken, I don't like that it scares me, it reminds me of my dad when he got drunk and I heard Nicole say to Dr Young hadn't we better eat and he said Ed's got the sandwiches. She said we'd better eat what we'd got otherwise he'd have vomit slopping all over the floor of the coach on the way back. Why did you let them bring alcohol anyway? She laughed she didn't seem to care, but Dr Young looked worried but he didn't say anything. It would have been lovely sitting there on the grass if things hadn't got a bit sort of wild. So we did eat the ginger bread which Nicole and Magda and Milosz had and the salad, and the students lay on their backs and talked and everything was calming down a bit when Ed and her came into sight and the students started being quite rude to Ed I thought, shouting to him, though Chris was cheeky he made a sort of joke about lunches and herbs and Ed noticed, and he chucked the sandwiches at them as if he was feeding the sea lions in the safari park which we took Tanya to once. Ed looked a bit stressed out and I got up to say something to him but he and Dr Young started eating sandwiches and I didn't want to disturb him. She looked stressed too and I heard Nicole ask where they'd been and how come they got lost. It wouldn't have happened if she hadn't been going on about it not being my first time on the mountains. And then suddenly it started to thunder. Everyone jumped up and started to run down to the cave I hate thunder. It's strange I can be quite bold about getting what I want, but loud noises frighten me, so I put my hands over my ears and eyes and stood still. Then Ed rescued me, he and Dr Young rushed back and carried me into the cave, it was horrible every time there was lightning I screamed I couldn't help it just came out of my mouth and I couldn't stop because they were holding my arms and I couldn't get my hands over my mouth and I was shaking and shivering. When it stopped they had to carry me out of the cave. It was like that catharsis that the lecturer talked about in Leeds, you feel so much pity and terror for the tragic hero you feel emptied out. I felt emptied out after the storm all my worries about uni and not getting on with her and upsetting Ed were gone and I felt light. I hadn't brought a rain coat so I went back in the coach with Nicole and I said what a day it had been and she said I had done brilliantly. I wrote a little note when I got back to our studio, I like to be in touch with people after an outing to make sure they know I had a good time and that I like them, I wrote a little note to her saying what a wonderful woman she was.

Brockenspectre

Vacation

After the students left and the university shut, I went to visit my son in Sheffield and my daughter in Warwick. Now I no longer tried to include Ed, they were thawing, and even managed to enquire about him. It was a stilted enquiry, but at least it was an enquiry.

Then Ed and I went to the States so he could spend time with Tom. We rented a house on the coast of Maine, where I could stay while Ed came and went – to a conference in Seattle, and another in Kansas. He spent a week in Massachusetts, bringing Tom back for a brief spell with us. Ed was so proud of him – he had some of Ed's seriousness and most of his mother's looks and was already as tall as Ed, but better fashioned, his feet and hands less large and his eyesight perfect – it made me want to cry.

North of Portland, Maine was beautiful. I loved the way the grey rock entered the sea, the way the clear water ebbed and flowed so quietly. I loved the trees that shielded the house from the road, even though I didn't love the poison ivy growing beneath them. I loved the glassed-in porch where I hung the swimwear to dry, and the sloping floorboards in the bedroom.

I knew I was being romantic. I knew the US wasn't like that, it was as poor and harsh as anywhere else in the world, but the first time I went there, for Ed to introduce me to Tom, the US bred in me an anticipation I found hard to explain. Ed and I descended from the New York train onto the platform – it wasn't even a station – sole passengers in the long level sunshine of the empty Massachusetts afternoon.

There was a promise, as if I were nineteen. Not as if. The promise was the same as when I *was* nineteen, the promise of adventure.

The next year, Ed and I went in late winter, around the time of Tom's birthday. One night there was an ice storm. In the morning every twig on each tree was cased in glass which tinkled at the faintest stir, and I had the same feeling. The trip was a scant week, so I turned my excitement down like the page of a book to be revisited, but the States said to me this was where I belonged, where I should be.

For five short weeks I pretended, yet there was risk in the pretence – going back I would be sad, like when I was woken from a dream.

Hour after hour I basked on a smooth boulder above the tiny beach. One morning as I lay there, face down, the sun crawling up my spine, I was reminded of my mother and another hot beach, the scene of my mother's destiny. I got up, swam, towelled off and went back to work. I wrote the story about her which I had begun in March, the day you entered my life.

Ed and I came back to find you had written to us both separately. There were eight postcards for me and a large brown envelope for him. While he listened to his phone messages he signalled to me to open the envelope. I tipped a shoal of cards out. His were closely covered with writing and were addressed "To Ed", like greeting cards.

The ones to me began "Dear Miriam". Mine were dated – two for each of the first four weeks of our vacation in Maine. They were intimate, as though they were written to a close friend. They gave me a breakdown of what you had been doing. In the first week you worked at the garden centre and in the pub and joined a book club. Also, as you were walking past the allotments one day, you got talking to a man who invited you to join the Allotment Society. It was another way to get to know people, and you liked to be part of several social groups. At the weekend you went to Cockermouth with Graham. The card was posted there.

There was more of the same in the second week. The book club was doing a Kate Atkinson novel. You enjoyed the detail and, as I knew, you loved history. At the weekend you and Graham went to Maryport, which you compared unfavourably to Whitby – it didn't have the atmosphere or the fun. Of course not. Maryport was run-down, without Bram Stoker to compensate.

The third week – the week I was on my own in Maine while Ed was in Massachusetts with Laura and Tom – was bad. At the garden centre you'd told off a kid for chucking stones into the ornamental pond. The parent complained to the manager, who in turn told you off in front of the kid. Or so you say. You flipped and lost your temper, telling him how much stress you were under and where to put his job. This caused a set-to with Graham about money, but you and he never really fell out because he was so patient.

I didn't know why you were revealing such personal details. Unless you wrote the card immediately after you'd had the argument, to exonerate yourself by your confession.

The fourth week was better. The Co-op needed a temp while one of their assistants was off and, because of your experience in the Co-op on the estate in Leeds, you were taken on. The book club and everyone at the Allotment Society were reassuring about the garden centre. They were certain the manager hadn't thought you were out of order. You seemed disappointed. As if you wanted them to be more indignant on your behalf. You'd bought me a "little present" from the Allotment Society sale which you would give me the next time we met. There was no postcard for what was our final week in the States. Maybe you had gone on holiday too.

Meanwhile, Ed inspected the contents of the more than twenty cards he had received. His expression progressed from the quizzical to the impatient, but all he said was, 'She's a bit volatile.' He swept them into an untidy deck, and then shuffled them back into the envelope, neither offering to show them to me nor asking to see the ones I had been sent.

'I'd better go into the office and find out what's been going on.'

'We've just flown in overnight – is it necessary?'

'I've got to keep awake to avoid jet lag. I won't be long – you can get sorted out here.'

I gathered my cards together, putting a rubber band around them. Did you want me as a friend? I wasn't sure. Your revelations seemed a ploy to get me on side, but for what I didn't know. I tucked in the note you sent after the picnic, went into Tom's room and shoved the whole lot to the back of my desk drawer. Apart from the envelope, now askew on Ed's semi-permanent mound of papers on the dining table, the flat had the dusty tidiness of being unoccupied. His going to the admin offices made me realise that I had become less settled here rather than more. While we were in the States his commitments were his choice, I was free to be me and it was like when we first met. I wished he was less single-minded. His dedicated acceptance of his role, and the undeviating routine of campus life, was beginning to feel like a trap.

The next day was Saturday. We stayed in bed. I made tea and we drank it. Ed made coffee and we drank that also. Eventually we showered and Ed went down to the entrance hall to see if there had been any post. When he returned he was holding two more envelopes.

'Hild?'

He smiled. 'She does make a habit of it. Good thing they aren't emails or phone calls.'

He opened the larger envelope and took out a birthday card. 'Bit late' he said, 'but how kind.' He opened the smaller one and behind his glasses his eyes widened.

'What does she say?' I asked, as I beat the batter for our pancakes.

'She says she hopes the fact I haven't responded to her cards, and that there were so many of them, doesn't mean she has discommoded me.'

'Discommoded? What an odd word to use.'

'The letter has an odd feel.'

'Can I see it?'

Ed handed the letter to me. It was on lined paper, the kind newsagents sometimes stock. You addressed him formally.

"Dear Dr Gallagher, I hope you won't mind me writing to you again. I feel I must apologise for writing so much to you in the last weeks, I hope you haven't felt pestered by me, you said when I bumped into you up at Administration that you didn't feel pestered, it was my right to write to you, but as you haven't answered any of the cards I just wonder if that's what you really mean. Maybe secretly you do feel a little bit hunted but because you are such a good and disciplined teacher you would not even allow yourself to feel that, but deep down you do. I just want to say that I wrote to you because it has been such an amazing time discovering this wonderful part of England which I know you love so much that I felt I had to share it with you as you were the one who helped me so much by letting me be taught by Miriam. Anyway that's all I wanted to say. Once again I hope I haven't annoyed or discommoded you. Yours faithfully, Hild Whittaker."

'Isn't this a complaint – she hopes you're not annoyed because you haven't answered her, and she's letting you know . . . Didn't you tell her you'd just received them when you saw her?'

Because Ed did see you. He'd shrugged it off but it sounded to me like you were lying in wait.

'Yes.'

'And what did you say when she wondered if you felt pestered?'

'"No more so than usual". It was a joke.'

'I don't think Hild's got a sense of humour – at least not your kind.'

'She'll get over it. She'll have too much to think about with the start of term and her course – and she's going to be a grandmother soon. Her daughter is pregnant. She's called Tanya.'

'I know she's called Tanya.'

'She told me yesterday. She's just found out.'

For the first time he was disquieted. He pushed the letter to one side and attacked his breakfast. Despite the maple syrup and the crisp bacon, these were Scottish drop scones, not American pancakes. Ed was back at work, I was back in England, the pretence was over, but I had become aware the promise of adventure could lead to infidelity just as easily as an affair.

Punto de vista

Classes began, though I had no students to teach. You had your own group of friends among the undergraduates and no longer needed me – if you ever did – and made this apparent by not getting in touch to give me the present you'd bought. The one time I saw you in the canteen, when I was having lunch with Ed, you waved, but I suspected it was Ed you were waving at. Yet when I met you in the Co-op you greeted me warmly. You told me you were working in the garden centre again – Andy, the manager, had taken you back – but you just did Sundays, and you were doing Tuesday nights as before in the Royal Oak. Gray came along too and was well-liked by its quiz team. You were at the allotments on Saturdays, but I didn't know what you did there – helped other people garden I suppose – and you'd dropped the book club because you had too much other reading. What Graham did, apart from the quiz, I didn't find out.

About your varied commitments, Ed said, 'That's quite a load', about Graham, 'What's not to like?' He was so busy he was scarcely aware of anything unrelated to the university.

Autumn progressed, and housing problems surfaced amongst the students. The summer had ended with high winds, flash floods and then persistent rain. Complaints about damp and mould creeping up the corners of their walls weren't part of Ed's brief, but as co-ordinator of student welfare they were frequently routed through to him.

One of the students to come to see him was you. Ed gave the standard advice – ventilate and heat. You didn't seem convinced, but you didn't argue, and Ed hoped you went away fairly satisfied. Having signed you off his books in the spring, he didn't want you back on them – you were now the responsibility of Jeff and your other lecturers.

His hope was not realised. You returned the next day saying Graham was in a right state over fuel costs. Ed went through your basic expenditure, an action well beyond his remit – I felt embarrassed for you and Graham having your budget examined – and sent you away, sure he had sorted you out. From then on he received a note, an email or a phone call from you about something every other day, then every day, then sometimes twice a day. You began turning up to see him. He would go to get a coffee and find you sitting in the corridor. There was always a query or a difficulty you needed to discuss with him and he could not refuse to talk to you because you were always on the verge of tears. On one occasion you were crying. He said he spent more time on bolstering you than all the rest of his charges. After a while he took to leaving his office door ajar, doing low grade administration as he listened to you, so there would be no doubt in anyone's mind as to why you were there.

You wrote to Francesca. You weren't able to afford to heat your flat. Francesca was perturbed. Most deans of educational institutions do not get direct appeals like this, but she was prepared to see what they could do. You were already in receipt of a laptop, courtesy of a university charity, but Ed found a hardship fund, specific to the campus, designed for single mature students with dependent children. As there was no one filling the category, he and Francesca raided it for what Francesca termed a "not inconsiderable sum". When she wrote to you to tell you of this she took the opportunity to advise you to use the Library for your studies. It would reduce the cost of your utilities. She was dismayed to receive a reply thanking her for the money but saying you found it difficult to concentrate in the Library.

However, getting the money must have pacified you, for you were no longer permanently on Ed's doorstep. This didn't indicate there weren't grounds for concern. Relayed to Ed as student mentor, you were causing unease in other areas. You were renowned for wanting to please, but weren't reliable. Your work was late, often not quite finished, the novel skimmed, the criticism half-read. There was always, an excuse – you had to do an extra shift in the pub so you could buy baby clothes, the Library didn't have the book, or your laptop was playing up or you hadn't been able to access the Wi-Fi.

Then you missed several classes to go and see the pregnant Tanya. Even though Ed had been avoiding contact with you as far as possible, he was annoyed when, courtesy of Reception, I told him about this visit. He considered you telling Reception was a sure way for everyone to get to know about it. I didn't see why you going to Leeds, or you informing Reception of your whereabouts in case someone needed to get in touch with you, or why anyone knowing about where you were, was problematic. Ed, however, thought you were presuming too much. While he was concerned for his students, they should behave according to the correct protocol, which didn't include treating the staff as members of one's family. I pointed out the campus was small and somewhat isolated. For some people, their colleagues and the students were their family. Ed disagreed. I said he was being inconsistent and his view rigid – I didn't say that when he was left without wife or child the college had stood in for his family. It was almost, but not quite, an argument. I learned more. While the ostensibly motherly women in Reception – they were too acute for that – felt you would settle down once Tanya's pregnancy was over, they also knew about earlier financial crises. There had, they said, been a shared ownership mortgage which could only be sorted by selling up, and credit cards used for trips to Paris and Barcelona.

I passed on their optimism to Ed, but I didn't tell him about the money. It might be unfair to you and I was trying very hard to be fair. Also, you'd never talked to me of places other than Whitby and Liverpool, and how you hated Leeds, nor mentioned owning your flat. Though I was taken aback at how indiscreet you were. I'd have thought you might keep such things private. It was as if your adoption of the ancillary campus staff was part of your waywardness, symptomatic of your flip-flopping between being independent and dependence. I began to wonder if Ed was right – you should keep your personal life separate from your student life.

Near our respective birthdays in early October – you didn't send me a card, perhaps you didn't remember, but it had stuck in my mind – Tanya's baby, a boy, was born. You were thrilled by this new grandson. Over the next few days your excitement was relayed to me by an elderly gardener I met as I walked past the allotments, the vicar when I took an astonished look at the pagan riot of the church's harvest decorations, the butcher, the librarians, and Anna at the Co-op, who you'd worked with in the summer and who was expecting her own baby. I heard the news, it goes without saying, from Reception. I heard it, more surprisingly, from Nicole. How she had found out I didn't know, and as I had just got off the train from Edinburgh which she was just about to catch to London, the conversation was limited to her, 'Have you heard, about Hild's grandchild?' and my, 'Yes'. I heard it from the women in the canteen. I even heard about it from Ed. In the past few months you had taken into your confidence as many people as I had become acquainted with in what was now the third anniversary of my arrival on campus.

The next week I heard the news from you yourself. I was waiting for Jeff's workshop in the Thornthwaite Room and you breezed through the door, your smile radiant.

'Did you know I was a grandmother, Miriam?'

You didn't look old enough. Despite your silver hair, the flesh on your neck and face was that of a young woman, firm and with a glow.

'Yes. Congratulations.'

You were happy and expansive as you told me how proud you were of your daughter. You told me about the labour, thirty-six hours, which seemed to me to be rather long, but you said such a length of time was not unusual in the first births of teenage mothers. You told me how much the baby weighed, two and a half kilos, which seemed to me to be rather light, but the weight was apparently acceptable. You promised to show me pictures.

I could be glad for you, as I was happier. I'd got over the dislocation of returning from the States, I'd had a good weekend with my daughter, and I was writing.

'It's brought me and Tanya together.'

I must have looked vague because you said with emphasis, 'Having a baby, Miriam, you'll see when your daughter has one.'

Had you trumped me in this, like you had over my primary school?

'That won't be for a long time.'

'No? I wanted Tanya to go to college, she's very good at computers and designing, but she said she was sick of school. Now I'm really pleased she's got Liam, and she'll have plenty of time to go later, like me.'

Then you glanced at the Della Robbias above the

picture rail and your mind switched from Tanya to them.

'My Gran was a Catholic. She used to love Mary. She said Mary knew what it was to have a baby.'

I stared up at their faces. I didn't know what period they were – baroque? I didn't think I liked the baroque, though when I first heard Bach played in a church full of white and gold angels in Munich I understood the reason for organ music. I didn't care for the Della Robbias much, whether they were baroque or not.

'Are you a Catholic too, Hild?'

'No.'

'Mary knew what it was to have her son murdered.'

You leapt back as if I'd hit you. There were sudden tears in your eyes.

I covered my shock, saying, 'I wonder why they've been left here.'

'What?'

'The Madonnas. They're not antiques – if they were, the university is so broke they would have sold them – but they must be worth something.'

I hoped my explanation would calm you. I didn't want a repeat of the experience in my flat.

It was an effort, but you said, 'Who left them here?'

'The boarding school.'

'School?'

'The one evacuated here in the second world war.'

'War?'

I wasn't reaching you. I checked my watch. Jeff and the others were late.

'I wonder why they put them up in a dining room. Maybe they used it as a chapel as well.'

You stood there so helpless, so confused, I felt I had to do something. The Madonnas. Knowing my action could be regarded as bizarre, yet I had to divert you from your distress. I carried my chair to the wall below the Madonnas, and got onto it.

'Let's look at them close up.'

You copied me. Near to, they were more impressive. The depth of colour and the thickness of the glaze took away their sickliness, made them solid. Each idealised duplicate became different, was somehow a real woman with her own potential for sorrow.

You touched the one in front of you with your finger and I heard the stirrings of curiosity in your voice, 'Why are there three of them?'

As I said, 'I've no idea,' the door opened and the rest of the group, taking A4 pads from their bags and cases, came in.

'What are you two up to?' Jeff hurried after them.

'Examining the Della Robbias. Thanks to Hild I've seen how beautiful they are. Are they baroque?'

Jeff gaped at me. He clearly thought I'd said something idiotic.

'Miriam. Please. The Renaissance.'

'I didn't know – I'm not an artist.'

'Neither am I, but I know my Bosch from my Bach.'

You looked enquiring.

'It's a pun – nearly.'

You smiled, but I didn't know whether it was in response to Jeff or me, or a reflex.

Jeff leant back in his chair and stretched his legs in easy authority.

'Right, so far we've spent this autumn looking at how to write a life. By now all of you should have done a short bit about their childhood. Who's going to read their work today?'

Most of us, today all of us, were there on a voluntary

basis. No one said anything. I didn't remark on the fact we had been exploring life writing for longer than this.

I lowered my eyes to the table. For the first time I noticed there were fork marks along its rim either side of where I was sitting. One of the girls must have pricked it, like a pie crust, while she was waiting to receive or leave the meal. Perhaps they weren't allowed to talk. Or she had no friend to talk to.

'Come on,' Jeff said, 'There is no sense in attending a workshop unless you're prepared to share what you've written. Remember, to get published you've got to agree to people reading your writing.'

Everyone laughed, but no one volunteered.

'We don't want to publish stuff about our lives. Would it be possible to write about something else, something less self-absorbed?'

Andrew was interested in crime writing and found making our inner selves public unpalatable, and unprofitable. 'Why don't you give us a title or a couple of words, something to act as a stimulus?'

His proposal was greeted enthusiastically by the group, only you looked disappointed.

I appreciated how difficult it was for Jeff, trying to teach a bunch of amateurs who could be awkward. Most of us knew we didn't have to do as we were told. On the other hand I didn't understand why he'd been insisting on autobiography, unless he thought using our own stories, material to hand so to speak, might make things easier for us.

'But what about today? Hild, have you got anything?'

Since you joined the group, Jeff had used you whenever there had been a hitch. He discovered you were willing to do things the rest of us ducked. It seemed that, despite your proven ability to get what you wanted, your sense of self-preservation was sometimes skewed. It had gone awry at the second session this autumn. You emailed everyone with an unrevised story for critique. For some reason your spelling and punctuation had regressed to pre-summer standards, and the responses were thorough. You didn't appear to mind, but Jeff shouldn't have taken advantage of your wanting to be noticed, which I was certain was the basis of your desire to please.

Before you could open your mouth and disclose what, judging from your hints, was a horrid background, I said, 'I've got something.'

Jeff knew I'd been avoiding this moment since the last time my work was discussed. He was amused. 'This is a pleasure, Miriam.'

Often, I dreamt I walked in the middle of a group of men and women, all of them unknown, along a concrete jetty which stuck out into a lake. Not a lake, not as friendly as a lake, a reservoir. I was pushed from the centre to the edge of the group. The water, too close, threatened. I had the same feeling now. I would rather not throw myself into the experience of reading my work, though I knew a tiny part of me did want to, but to save you, I would.

'What's it called?' you asked.

'It's a Spanish title – "*Biblioteca*".'

'What's that mean?' You were petulant. I had taken the focus away from you.

'It means "Library".'

'What library?'

'The school library.'

. . . The library held no fears for her.

Not like the middle of the studio when she was asked to come forward to perform pirouettes or pas de chats.

Then she stood, paralysed on the edge of the room, afraid to commit her feet to something she was never certain of them doing. Eventually, she obeyed, but she felt she would become dizzy, would fall over in the pirouettes, unable to follow the direction to 'flick the head but keep the eyes on the same spot', and she knew her pas de chats could not achieve the lightness of those of the rest of the class, whose neat bodies flitted through the air, satiny pink slippers landing with an almost soundless tap on the rosined floor.

When she landed, their teacher, his tights revealing his swelling thigh muscles, cried, 'Ligeramente. Lightly, Miriam, lightly,' and she was forced to say, 'Sorry, sorry, Señor Ramos'.

The other girls, who called the teacher el oso because of the black pelt they saw curling above the neck of his leotard, and the hair silkily flowing down his arms, giggled at her – not without sympathy – but she was too tall to be a ballet dancer. At sixteen she was as tall as el oso. Yet she knew she could dance. Her jive, practised alone in the living room, had a loose expertise.

The library was hers. It gave her satisfaction to arrange – she preferred to say it in Spanish, "arreglar" had a feeling of order – the books on the dark shelves. It was a pleasure, a stack held in her left arm, to make spaces amongst the dull-coloured spines for the one she was putting back.

She'd wrested it in a power struggle, from her best friend, Nina. Miriam was granted the library. Nina got to be head girl.

The school used it as a lecture theatre when Sister Serena came to tell them about her work in the poor barrios.

Afterwards, as she guided Sister back to the entrance hall, Sister asked what her name was and said, 'Have you ever thought you had a vocation?'

'No.'

'To teaching, perhaps?'

Miriam shook her head. She had no vocation, not even to teaching. She liked books and she liked the authority the library gave her. The younger girls asked her to recommend stories, came before and after school to do their preparation in the silence she imposed. She tried to nurture their tastes, tried to interest them in the classics. At least, she tried to interest them in Dickens. Miriam had gulped all of him down, or thought she had. *Nicholas Nickleby*, *A Tale of Two Cities*, *David Copperfield*. Later, when she was grown up, when she read *Bleak House*, she wondered what it was she had read. They didn't want Dickens. Difficult books in English were not for young girls.

The older ones? They didn't want Dickens either, or the old-fashioned books imported from England years before which Miriam also gobbled up – the imperial red, white and blue of British life in the colonies of Africa, weird histories of the icy far north, family sagas set on the plains of Canada.

They weren't interested. They had no desire to escape to other countries, no wish to lose themselves in times past. They wanted romances, or found their stories in the things that happened to them in the evenings and weekends, when they went to the beach with the young men from the boys' school down the road to play volleyball and lie together in the sand. Or when they invaded the local dances, or lounged in cafés until late at night, eating ice cream and drinking cola and soda.

One afternoon, the door opened, banging against the shelves, and Nina came in with another girl. They had piles of books in their arms. They had come to study. Only they didn't. They leaned on a table and talked. For quite a long time. It started to annoy Miriam, and when the girls became distracted, stopped their reading and their homework and began to whisper to each other, she went over and asked them, finger to her lips, to be quieter.

Nina said in a loud voice, 'Calme, Miriam,' and smiled at the other girl.

Miriam lost her temper and shouted, 'Get out.'

Nina raised meaningful eyebrows, and they left, shutting the door very, very carefully.

The girls stared at her. Avoiding their eyes, she moved around her library, finding books, putting them away, instructing herself, 'Calme te, Miriam, calme te . . .'

There was a long silence.

Finally Andrew said, 'It appears to flow.'

I hadn't expected him to enjoy it, but Deborah chipped in, 'It has authenticity,' and I was demoralized. She was a poet and I thought she might have appreciated it. Her description of the piece as authentic suggested it was dull.

'It's better than the thing you wrote about the tea cosy, Miriam,' Jeff said. His smile was tepid rather than approving.

'Tea cosy?' Both your early happiness, and the misery caused by my remark about the Della Robbias, vanished. Your response was avid, like when you held the photo of my parents.

'Miriam's three hundred words on the horrors of tea cosies and ceilidhs.'

Was that why Jeff was suspicious of me? My indifference to certain aspects of English life, some bits of which Jeff rated highly – ceilidhs and folklore – was insufficiently disguised?

'Shall I read mine, Jeff?' Your own work made you expectant.

I was appalled. Had I laid my life open to the boredom of my listeners to find I hadn't rescued you, that you were determined on martyrdom? I looked across the table at Jeff, my sometime colleague as well as my workshop leader, and gave the tiniest shake of my head. He shouldn't allow you to do it. He ignored me. Either he was stupid or arrogant. Or I'd got it wrong.

The account of your early life in Liverpool with your mum, dad, and three little sisters was as bad as I had expected, a tale of poverty and violence. It got worse – you were intimating serial incest. I watched the whole group freeze, not daring to move under the relentless flow of detail all the more horrifying because it was delivered in such a matter-of-fact way. We looked at our pads of paper, looked at the window blinds, looked at the door, as if looking would somehow realise our desire to be somewhere else, all of us now wishing we'd agreed to read our own work. Frantic to escape, I looked at the Madonnas. They hadn't been put here for an aesthetic or spiritual purpose. They had been put here to remind the girls of their mothers. To remind them they weren't alone, as you had made each one of us alone, reading into the void of our discomfort.

Coming to the end, you added, your accent now so thick with emotion I found it difficult to understand. 'So, that's why I think of Gray as my prince, he rescued me from all that. And I wanted to read it out before I went to see my daughter, Tanya, and Liam, sort of get it out of the way.'

I realised I shouldn't have tried to rescue you. Like you and Graham arguing over money, and the confidences you had shared with Reception, this was a confession. Your childhood wasn't your fault, but confessing absolved you, and you intended achieving this absolution all along.

Jeff looked disconcerted. No wonder. He'd

miscalculated. He had to be hoping you hadn't grasped how much you'd exposed yourself.

He said, and for once he sounded tentative, 'Andrew may be right. For the next session you should undertake a more technical exercise. I don't think you've covered point of view, have you? Can you describe an incident from different points of view? Doesn't have to be long, a paragraph in first, second and third person.'

He was so unnerved he didn't ask if we understood him, while you were so engrossed in re-reading your work you didn't ask him for an explanation as you usually did. He left with a muttered goodbye.

Did all the four children have to sleep in one room? Did all this happen in the one room? For how long – until you were teenagers? And after? During the day were you together all the time, except when you were at school? Did you go out to get away from each other? How did people live, thirty years earlier? I didn't know. I'd just arrived in England, sent back to get a degree from an English university. Even setting aside the possibility of incest, to live in a university, however bleak the walkways, whatever the stink of the muck spread on the fields encircling the halls of residence, wasn't the same as being one of six crammed in a two-bedroomed flat, in a high rise in Liverpool with broken lifts. I couldn't conceive how you had managed to come so far.

You didn't seem to comprehend you'd made us, your listeners, voyeurs, complicit, ourselves exposed by your revelations. You declared blithely you would bring your novel, a fictionalised account of your grandmother's life, to the next session. Deborah, Andrew, and the rest had to be – were – sympathetic, but your disclosures intimidated them. Not staying to talk, they followed Jeff out, and over the next weeks numbers diminished, until the only ones remaining were you and me, plus Angie and Suzanne, a couple of undergraduates absent on the day, who, unconcerned, continue to attend. Though the secrets you divulged about your grandmother were as dismaying, they could be more easily handled, as they were at one remove and Angie and Suzanne didn't care. They took the story at face value – it was about your crazed grandmother.

If it was your grandmother. Because I was suspicious, just as I was over Hallin Fell. You wanted the limelight too much. Had your autobiographical piece been a nudge to make the group wonder about the identity of your fictional protagonist? Yet why not? Jeff said fiction was made up, but wasn't dishonest, though I believed it could be. I wondered what Jeff thought, but he was too busy plugging the holes in his own shortcomings to worry about your honesty. His handling of the situation had been poor, and even though the workshop was, for most of us, voluntary, he insisted, to cover himself, that from then on work must be emailed to him in advance, so what we had to critique was chosen by him.

It was around that time you began to bombard me with messages. They thanked me for what you had learned – from me. You cited various comments I had made about books and writing, telling me how much you had picked up from them. You were grateful for the generosity I showed you in the summer by teaching you, when I didn't have to. You praised my "graciousness". I didn't know why you chose the word, and I'd have loved to accept the compliment, but it made me uncomfortable. I knew my own duplicity. I was, secretly and frequently, more than ungracious about you.

As the messages continued to pour in I knew you had been – were – downstairs delivering them. I received them every day. I dreaded finding them in the letterbox. Sometimes they came in the morning, sometimes in the afternoon. And, though I spent most of my time at my computer, somehow, somewhere, I saw you every day. I could avoid you neither on the campus nor in the high street. It was such a tiny community I shouldn't have found this strange, but I did. You would approach, hold on to my sleeve, or sometimes my elbow, standing so close your body almost touched mine.

I might have described you to a stranger as ebullient, but it wasn't the right word. You were not ebullient, you were garrulous, and, in an awful way, devoted. You told me more about your life before you came here, more about your family. You empathised with the scraps of my life which I felt obliged, as Ed's partner and a member of staff, so by definition supportive and caring, to offer up in return. Your attention made me lose my head. I avoided going to the canteen but when I did I bought a sandwich rather than soup, forgot my reason for going into the post office. I didn't understand why it was you wanted to talk to me. I didn't understand what was happening. I started to wonder if I was making up the messages and the meetings.

One day, Magda and Milosz came to the flat for an informal tutorial. It gave me the opportunity to ask if they were in contact with you. To find out if I was imagining your onslaught. Yes, they saw you often. Like them, you worked quite late in the Library. I was on the verge of asking if you had changed your mind about studying in libraries, but it was inside knowledge which I wasn't supposed to have.

I asked if they knew what you did apart from your studies. You belonged to Jeff's theatre group, and after rehearsals drank in the pub with them. On top of the social life there was your paid work, and your involvement with the town.

'I don't know how she do it,' Milosz said, 'it is

exhausting to me.'

'And she is married, would Gray-ham not mind?' Magda said. 'Have you met him, Miriam?'

'Only at the Founder's Day lecture, and the fire siren went off just . . . '

'Just?' Magda prompted me.

'. . . just as I made a stupid comment about the lecture needing to be leavened with an unexpected event. Like a fire. It distressed Graham.'

Milosz laughed with real amusement. 'Someone took you for true?'

'"For real" – rather took my remark at "face value". I hope not.'

'Have you seen the photos of Liam, Miriam?' Magda asked. 'She has shown me them one time.'

'No.'

'She has not been to see him. She says she will go when the baby is older, not quite so new. To give her daughter time to get used to look after him.'

Magda examined her coffee cup as if trying to tell your fortune. It was clear she thought this a curious way for a new grandmother to behave.

You were doing too much. It explained the staff's disquiet over the scantiness of your work, but not your sudden enthusiasm for me. My distaste didn't lessen. I took the recent notes, the note you sent after the picnic, and the cards from the summer which I'd put to the back of my desk drawer, and slung them into one of Ed's old box folders. I stuffed it under the spare clothes in our wardrobe. I took it out. I didn't want you in our bedroom. I hid the folder in the hall among the oversize books left behind by Laura about European architecture. Ed didn't look at them so he was unlikely to find it.

Abruptly, you switched your attention back to Ed. There was a flood of texts, followed by phone calls to Ed on the landline. As abruptly, you switched back to me. Every time you rang I asked if you wanted to speak to Ed and every time you said you were phoning to talk to me. You rang to ask me a question about a novel or a poet. You rang to tell me about something you had read which you thought would help me with my short stories, or was it a memoir, Miriam? You rang to tell me your self-revelation in the workshop was the best thing you could have done, you were writing loads. You would get your degree, drag your family out of their present hardship, become a writer. Like you, Miriam. You were excited, buoyed up by the future you envisaged.

And yet. In the summer, your choice of clothes was sometimes odd, the dresses you wore more fitting to someone younger, but you were pretty, very pretty. In fact, when you told me how lucky you were, how, whenever you needed them, you acquired saviours, and added, with a creamy laugh, that, inevitably, they fell in love with you, I believed you. For you exuded the sexuality, both innocent and knowing, which I observed at the first class.

And yet. When I encountered you during this period you were unkempt. You wore jogging pants which were limp, grubby and too long, the hems ragged, you had on ancient trainers and a shabby fleece, you looked as deprived as you said you'd been. Then you were smart, but your smartness was inappropriate. In the middle of a working day you had on an evening skirt. On both occasions your hair was sweaty, the colour of unpolished pewter, like it was the day of the picnic. Your manner was different, you were less talkative, less enthusiastic. I was disturbed by the way you looked, but depending on what I was doing and how I felt, I too might fling on a scruffy sweater, an old pair of trousers. I too could be subdued and prone to self-doubt.

My confidence in my work had wavered. I managed dribs and drabs of memoir, but couldn't make it cohere. If I tried to make it sequential it became a trudge. If I tried to write in snippets I was not able to connect them and the writing collapsed. I called my daughter. She told me not to carry on if it was causing me such a problem. I recognised that she and my son were adults and weren't troubled about my past. Their father divorced from me, their mother. If my daughter couldn't have her father and me together, she didn't want to know. I felt her lack of interest was a punishment.

It forced me to think about my father. Transferring to the Santiago office when I left for Europe. My mother dying. My father relocating permanently to Chile. Marrying Teresa. Becoming father to Teresa's virtually grown children. I had visited him a few times, but I hadn't liked going. Pinochet's rule and what came after didn't affect my father. Despite Will and I being born and brought up in Argentina, my father's excellent Spanish and his new family, he was English. I couldn't ignore the politics. I might be an exile in England, but in Chile I was a visitor, and I felt I was there in bad faith. I didn't know what Will thought, it wasn't something we raised in our letters. We kept those light, there were too many miles, and years, between us to conduct real discussion.

He was determined to be a gaucho. Homesick at boarding school, he read Hudson's *Allá Lejos y Hace Tiempo* many times, and all he wanted was to be on horseback, or in a truck, out in the camp. We met, last met, in Heathrow. I was nineteen, on my way to university in England. He, at eighteen, was going home, and then to Santa Rosa and the pampas. In the thrill of being adult, with the optimism of siblings who'd had too few opportunities to be with each other, but who cared for each other deeply, we made a pact to meet up somewhere, in some airport, every five years. With a languages degree, it would be easy for me to travel anywhere. Though a gaucho's wages weren't enormous, over the five years, he would be able to save enough for the flight.

A gaucho who married young and had four children couldn't save money for flights, and after teaching in France I too married, had children, ceased to travel. We didn't meet, but sent letters every month. He probably hadn't kept them, it wasn't in his character to hoard, especially bits of paper. Now our contact was by email. It was more immediate but also more sporadic and brief.

I sometimes wondered if he'd kept the photograph albums I'd sent from Chile after my father died. Simon had shown himself uninterested in being guardian of my family's past, and someone in every family needed to keep the memories.

I always found late October and the beginning of November alarming, thought something would go wrong, a silliness left over from having young children and worrying about them being out on their own in the earlier and earlier dusk. The irony was that after the rain and wind at the start of the autumn the weather was good, so good Ed said it reminded him of the fall. There was sun during the day, frost at night, and an absence of wind. For me, the warmth of the days and the quiet nights should have made things easier, yet they didn't. The weather mocked me. Your phone calls taunted me.

In some ways they should have been no more difficult to handle than the notes. Unlike those, which I found impossible to destroy, they left no evidence, but your voice was corrupting. I could not miss the sycophancy. If it was sycophantic. Maybe, and I didn't want to think it, the voice was of some kind of desire. Whatever it was, there came a time where I hated to pick up the phone. A time when hearing your name made me feel sick. A time where I was unkind to you, and you – was your response masochistic? – forgave me, saying, 'I know what it is, Miriam, you must be having a bad day'. I hated being forgiven, most of all by you.

I didn't understand why you affected me, why I wasn't able to shake off your persistence as your problem, not mine. Aware we shared some similarities, and a barely latent rivalry, I became obsessed, afraid our almost shared birth dates made us almost the same person. I woke sweating in the night and lay wondering what you were doing, what I would say next time I met you in order to drive you from me. I slept until nine, ten, eleven, in the morning. When I woke, my first thought was where I might meet you. It was such a small place. I drove to the supermarket on the outskirts of Penrith rather than chance running into you in the local shops.

Because I was so tired, I couldn't concentrate. I became certain you were preventing me writing. Every day I pushed my laptop away from me, put my head on my arms and slept. One day I dreamt I was clothed in white lace. I was the spider queen, and you and your daughter Tanya were crowning me, with a gossamer headdress. I roused myself with difficulty, forcing my eyes open, lines scored by my cable sweater criss-crossing my cheek. Spiders spin their webs from their own innards, their hundreds of offspring float away to breed, but in my dream you made me sterile. Not Tanya. You. You entrapped me in a role of sterility.

I decided I had to exorcise you. I would confront you. I would write about you. Using Jeff's point of view task I would write you out of my life. I would write from Jeff's point of view, from Ed's, from Nicole's, from further and further away, until you were gone. Until I was immune, and was able to hear your name without dread. That is what I decided.

Then every time I sat down to write, you rang me. By Friday I was desperate. Aside from one shopping trip, I hadn't been anywhere. All I'd done, all week, was answer your calls and roam around the flat. My watch chafed my wrist. I took it off. I looked out of the window. I gazed at the black cat sitting under the bird feeder in The Close. It gazed back at me with eyes so yellow that even from that distance I saw the dark slits of its pupils. Why did it come every afternoon, why not during the feeding flurry in the morning and the evening? How would I know if it did? In the morning I was asleep, by the evening I was too distracted to notice.

I had to begin. In the first person? In the third?

In your voice? If I didn't give you a chance to speak would I ever be free of you?

Hild. You said it was short for Hildegard, a poet nun in Germany, but that was a fantasy. How would a girl from Liverpool, even from a Catholic family, get to be called Hildegard? A poet nun? You wanted to be a poet, but nun? No, you'd made the whole thing up. You had shortened Hilda to Hild so you became someone different. It was a lie. Like pretending you cared for me. Like wanting an education. I'd become convinced you only wanted an education for the notice it earned.

Of course, with you as the subject I couldn't take the exercise to the workshop, but I didn't want to go anyway. I didn't want to see you. Have you forgive me. Be nice to me. Or be nasty, as I knew one day you would.

I couldn't show it to Ed either. Even disguised, he would recognise you. Whatever his feelings, I knew you aggravated him, he wouldn't let them get in the way of his professional dealings with you, get in the way of his work. This writing had to be secret. A secret between the "me" who was writing and the "you" I was writing about. For my eyes alone. That way I could pretend I was not trying to get rid of you. Because I knew the idea I could get rid of you by writing you out of my life was a delusion. A delusion as crazy as you were making me.

. . . Miriam regarded Hild from a distance as she talked to Jeff outside the Thornthwaite Room where Miriam was waiting for the workshop to start. Hild looked up at Jeff in a supplication and put her hand on his forearm. She supposed Hild thought the gesture was endearing her to Jeff, was somehow connecting her to him, but it didn't look endearing to Miriam. It looked as if she was forcing him to like her, to agree with her. Was she jealous? Not of Jeff, she and Jeff had a detached relationship. He was, after all, Ed's friend first and foremost. No, she wasn't jealous so much as irritated by the dishonesty of Hild's behaviour, the way everyone seemed to be taken in by it because of the special status she commanded as a mature – a needy – student. Miriam was sure there were other students just as needy as Hild, but they didn't flaunt their need so they didn't get the time, the money, the praise she demanded . . .

It didn't work. It didn't remove you, it merely revealed a lack of generosity in myself, a neediness of my own, a desire for attention, which I didn't like to acknowledge. Which I hadn't had to acknowledge until your intrusion into my life. Besides, it was too measured. It didn't express the fury and fear I felt. I did feel fear. Teaching you, and your refusal to submit to rules, showed me how constrained I was by the very education you were seeking. You made me fear I was mediocre. I was afraid, and so I was angry with you. I was also jealous. When you wanted to, you wrote well, and I was terrified you would make it, but not me. I was even more terrified that if one of us – you – didn't make it, then the other – me – wouldn't make it either.

If I wrote from your point of view, would that exorcise you?

. . . Gray says you are a very strong lady, Miriam, which is what I want to be. I don't have an exotic background, nor a good education like you, I haven't travelled in foreign countries, my mum and dad weren't rich, but I've got talent and I've got support. So many people support me, Miriam, I seem to attract such wonderful people, such wonderful friends, as you know because I tell you about them, from Anna at the Co-op, to Magda and Milosz and Nicole, and the ladies in the Library and at Reception. Then there's Jeff, who's teaching me so much, and Ed. He is not only my tutor but I think of him as my friend, and he is a counsellor as well, which I think makes him wise. You are a great lady, Miriam, but you are distant. Gray says you have a very strong handshake. You're different from the rest of us, probably because of your upbringing, but I expect you like to be different, seeing as how you want to be a writer. I want to be a writer too, that's why I am at uni, so I can catch up. I just have to be able to write, as you would say, "properly". . .

I'd written what I imagined you might write, an attempt undermined by not knowing what you thought. Saying I was "strong" and "great". They had a basis in fact. You'd said both those to me. There was truth in how you saw things, even though it was I who had written what you saw. I was different, though not that different. Except for the secretarial and domestic staff, everyone on campus was an offcomer. Graham did rub his hand after I'd shaken it when I met him, and smiled at you. I thought he was making fun of me. What I saw as you gushing, you needling me, I couldn't lay those at your door. It was your point of view from my viewpoint. My own *punto de vista.*

The exercise didn't remove you. It had the opposite effect. It brought you to life. Now I saw things as I imagined you seeing them and it made me wonder if, what to me was your dishonesty, was created by my inadequacy which made me unable to see other people's needs.

Would it work if I wrote as an omniscient author? The setting, Francesca Farrington's sedate sherry and cheese straws to mark the close of the Christmas term. Festive, but with an undercurrent. It would show me ignoring your attempts to ingratiate yourself by offering to help me hand the cheese straws around. Me, cold-shouldering you. It would show you getting the message, going back to Leeds with Graham, going back to Tanya and your grandson.

At midday, Ed returned to the flat. He had begun to check on me, anxious because I had stopped going out and was sleeping late. When he asked me what was wrong I said I was unwell. I didn't say you were the cause.

I told him I wanted to leave the workshop, it was getting me nowhere.

He said I wasn't to give up, it was one of the only ways, living on campus, for me to be independent of him, to be away from him. I didn't ask, why do we stay here? Instead I said numbers had dwindled. With no more than two or three of us it wasn't worth my going.

'Numbers aren't important. It's the quality which counts.'

'The quality is crap.'

'No, it's not. Not if your work is anything to go by.'

'What do you know about it? You're a scientist.'

'That's unfair, Miriam.'

'I can't go, I haven't written anything.'

'You wrote some bits in Maine – put one of them in.'

He left. Did the glass door rattle more than usual? He was trying to help and I didn't want to be helped. Not by him.

In the afternoon I picked a book from those stacked under the window, a rare present from Will which I'd had for several years, but not read. The date the novel opened was that day's date. Coincidence is always strange.

On occasions things happened to me which seemed to be omens, or portents, signs showing the way forward. The sorts of things which made the world halt.

Not the way it did if a child was lost and the trees around a house became a vast and more impenetrable wood as the evening deepened, though in daylight they were a stand of swaying pines in dry Surrey soil. Then, the world crashed, and I put on my shoes and gave orders to my daughter not to leave the house. I ran in one direction, my husband in the other, calling. My son and the world returned, but now the knowledge was always there. It was bricked up, yet behind the blindness of the brick there was the dark, and from time to time a wisp of it escaped.

Portents made me pause. They halted the world, but differently. They revealed the existence of another world.

I have dreamt when people were about to die... The note, which reassured me my course of action was the right one, was in the handwriting of my long gone father... Reflecting on my drive to work about the lack of security in schools, I later received word of a massacre.

These were messages. Messages like the one I saw written on the kitchen wall of a house Simon wanted to buy. Not there on the first visit, it was there on the second visit, the day after the row we had over the buying. The message told of someone else's murderous row.

Portents hinted of pattern. It was what I found in novels. A beginning, a middle, an end. Though the fiction I read now was bleaker, tougher, unravelled at either end, in the middle there was pattern, there was meaning. Fiction had taught me to press, to mould my life into a shape. Fiction was perilous. When the mould failed – when Simon no longer wanted me and I no longer wanted him – I was despairing, until I started to press and mould my life into another fiction, to find meaning in portents.

I lay on the floor, and read. The novel was about three women haunted by an imposter, a woman who was not who she seemed to be. After an hour I got up. It was a sign to me to continue. I knew what to do. I would write a novel. You were an imposter, not what you pretended to be. You would be my protagonist, but I would give you another name. After you told me you were called Hildegard I looked up the name and discovered it meant Heddi, cause of strife. I would call you Heddi, and Graham I would call Greg. In my novel I would destroy you. If you ever came to read it, you wouldn't know I was poisoning you, but I would.

I emailed Jeff the other piece I'd written in Maine – not my mother's story, that was too personal – and began to construct my plot.

Hallowe'en

After the turmoil of the previous week, my decision made me calmer. I began to be ashamed of allowing myself to become so miserable. Had I imagined your persecution, my confusion? The cautious manner in which Ed talked to me indicated I hadn't, even if it hadn't lasted as long as I believed. My walk to the Thornthwaite Room on Monday was placid, and I enjoyed watching the staff's smallest children, busy under the horse chestnut tree filling carrier bags to the brim with greasy conkers. They would be left to shrivel in the dust under their beds until the urgent need to find a water pistol rediscovered them on the first hot day of spring.

You sat on the steps outside the Library, dressed in black – black leggings and a tight black sweater. With the gold threads in your silver hair glinting in the sunshine, and your eyes half-closed, you looked sleepy and contented.

'Hi Miriam, do you think some of the others will be back this week?'

Although I'd regained some self control, I didn't want to talk to you. I didn't tell you Deborah said your disclosures and the quasi-authoritarian system Jeff had put in place had made her recoil. In any case your question was lazy and didn't demand an answer.

Angie and Suzanne strolled up, greeted us, and went on with their conversation, leaving me to absorb the autumn sun in silence and you to doze on the steps.

Jeff was already ten minutes late when Angie said, 'Should we go in?'

You got up and stretched, a protracted stretch. You

yawned, pushing one arm, followed by the other, above your head, your hands bending backwards like a mime artist's. Then you clasped them behind you and bent to the right, and to the left, exposing a line of pale stomach, with movements which were flexible and easy. Angie and Suzanne stayed put, fascinated by this display, until Jeff arrived.

Ushering us in, he said that as Angie and I had produced something based on our childhoods, he would use them today to wrap up the autobiographical element of the work. To allow each of us to approach our work objectively, he would read out the material.

Jeff started with Angie's encounter with her teacher on her first day at primary school. It was a touching account of a feisty little girl who wasn't naughty but had a clear understanding of how she wished to lead her life. It hurt me that her teacher felt her will had to be tamed. The discussion which followed was lengthy. Rather than focussing on the style of her writing it centred on how Angie could have remembered what had happened, how memory worked. Angie had to agree she'd got most of it from her mother and father.

Then Jeff turned to, "my mother bought a dog once".

There was silence when Jeff finished reading, similar to the one which greeted "*Biblioteca*".

I didn't know why everyone was silent. I wasn't so deluded as to think it was the silence which greets a great performance before turning into storming applause, but was it such a bad story? It wasn't a comedy, or a tragedy, or even a slice of history. It was doctored memory. Perhaps my daughter was right and that was the cause. My memories were significant to me alone.

In the end, rolling your r's – I knew you were

mimicking me, for I have never lost the Spanish 'r' – you announced, 'I feel sorry for the dog,' which destroyed any illusion of the story's pathos, eased the tension for Angie and Suzanne, and released Jeff into his role of workshop leader.

He asked, 'So how much of this actually happened? Is the dog's name real?'

'"Feo" is a real Spanish word.'

'Which translates as?'

'It means "ugly".'

'And your mother did bicycle back with it buttoned into her coat? And handed the care to you?'

'Yes.'

'I don't know where it's set,' Angie said. 'Somewhere foreign? You made it sound foreign, Miriam.'

With the knowledge you'd acquired from your classes with me, and the time you came to our flat, you said, 'It is foreign.'

'How do you know? Where does it say so?' Suzanne asked.

'We know because there are indicators in the text's vocabulary, the language used – "*estancia*" is a farm and "the camp" denotes the countryside in Argentina and Uruguay.' Jeff had done his homework.

'I thought "the camp" meant a campsite.' Suzanne giggled.

You asked, 'Isn't *maté* a sort of tea they drink, Miriam?'

'Yes.'

And went on, 'It does make it difficult for your reader if they don't know those words, doesn't it, Miriam?'

'I suppose it might . . .'

'Especially if there's nothing else to tell us where it is set, or what the people look like.'

'There is a clue, Hild. I talk about the rain of the southern Atlantic winter streaming off the red roofs of the villas.'

Jeff sighed. 'I think Hild is saying the detail is not sufficiently tangible – aren't you, Hild?'

'It does ramble on, doesn't it?' Your earlier sleepiness had disappeared.

'I wasn't able to see the girl,' Angie said.

'All those other dogs, the ones barking at the gates,' said Suzanne, 'and the rain on the red tiles, might be a rough estate in Manchester or somewhere.'

'No, it couldn't, on those estates the dogs run loose.'

No one attempted to argue. You knew what you were talking about.

'They don't have maids on estates like those either.' Angie threw me a conspiratorial smile. 'Did you really have a maid, Miriam?' The feistiness hadn't been beaten out of the little girl.

'Yes, until I left to come to England. I've not had one since.'

'I had an au pair when I was small.'

As you opened your mouth, Suzanne butted in, 'So did I,' and she and Angie began to exchange stories about growing up. Though I wasn't sure if Jeff was letting them continue with the flow of incidents in order to shield me, their intervention was deliberate.

There was no other word for it. You sulked.

When time was up Jeff reasserted his authority.

'Now you've all done something on your childhood, do you want to continue within the broad outline of autobiography, or move on?' He seemed to have forgotten about the point of view exercise he'd proposed.

'Why don't we all bring one of our photographs –

we could write stories based on them.'

'Good idea, Hild. It would combine autobiography with a new genre.'

'Does the photo have to be autobiographical?'

'No, but most photos, interesting photos, contain people, Miriam.' Jeff wasn't allowing any argument.

'I can bring one of my wedding,' you said.

I thought it strange you had brought your photographs with you. You told Ed you arrived here as a nomad, but bringing them revealed a desire to settle rather than merely study. Did you want to begin afresh? Did you think you would find a niche in this academic setting? Niches were few and highly coveted. They only went to those who had a specific talent or skill a university wanted.

'Right, next week bring in a photo to stimulate a narrative.'

'Not next week, Dr Young. Next week's Reading Week. Anyone else going to the Hallowe'en gig apart from me and Suze? I'm going as a goth. I'm going to make a costume.'

It was obvious Angie didn't intend to do a lot of reading.

'I'm going to Whitby.' Or you either.

Jeff's eyebrows contracted.

'Lots of goths in Whitby at Hallowe'en, Hild. Are you going to the Dracula thingy, the museum – all blackout and tunnels?' Suzanne's eyes gleamed.

'No.'

'Why not? Angie and I went two years ago. It's a great place.'

'I'm frightened of tunnels.'

Thunderstorms, the dark, tunnels. What else?

'Gray will hold your hand.' Was there a hint of a

smirk on Suzanne's face?

'Yes. No. I don't know.' You brightened. 'Me and Gray are going to stay with Brian and Tanya. It'll be the first time we see Liam.'

'Haven't you been yet?' According to Ed, Jeff was a devoted father, and his surprise was noticeable.

'No. I've been busy.'

Though Magda said you made a conscious decision to delay seeing the baby, you sounded defensive.

As a diversion I asked, 'What's Whitby like?'

'I'll write a description for you, Mirrie. Gray and me have a holiday there every year.'

The abbreviation of my name was deliberate, and amused Angie and Suzanne. I made the same mistake every time. Whenever I tried to protect you, you attacked.

'Shall I give it to you, Jeff?'

'I'll look forward to it.'

Late for his next class, Jeff dashed off, you went after him, and I followed, leaving Angie and Suzanne planning a project they had left to the last minute. I envied their uncomplicated attitude to their studies.

When we had to send Feo away, it wasn't only my brother who wept, but I couldn't admit it. To do so would be to recognise how sad partings made me.

You must have gone home and started on "Whitby" straightaway, because Ed discovered it in the letterbox when he came to check on me and have a post-lunch coffee. The handwriting was unmistakeable.

'Something for you from Hild.'

'I'll look at it later.'

I didn't. I avoided the kitchen, where it lay beside the coffee pot and the strainer full of grouts Ed had left.

In the evening he went straight into the kitchen

calling, 'Got to make myself some sandwiches – a meeting I forgot. Sorry.'

There were no sounds of opening the bread bin, getting out butter and lettuce. Instead Ed came into Tom's room where I was sitting at my desk.

'You haven't read what Hild sent you.'

'Too busy. Besides, I am no longer employed to read students' work.'

He was firm. 'You read Magda's and Milosz's. Hild is no different. She was your student too, Miriam. You must read it.'

I knew if I refused he'd ask me why, and the subject of you would begin again. If I read it to Ed he would act as buffer between us. He went back into the kitchen to defrost bread in the toaster and I followed.

"Whitby is my special place, I think each one of us has a special place and Whitby and Robin Hoods Bay well both of them are mine and Gray's special place. What is special about Whitby? Well first of all its by the sea and I am happiest when I am by the sea I feel energetic and I want to do things all the time. Gray says I am always doing things and it would be a good thing to do a bit less but its a different kind of thing. In Whitby and Robin Hoods bay I get up early every morning at about six o-clock and go across the path over the tops of the cliffs. The dew is on the grass and it tickles the sides of my feet and sends shivers up my calves and the back of my thighs. At six o'clock the sea is usually calm I don't know why, and I can see right out at the ships that have come from Tynemouth and are going to Holland. They crawl along the sea like beetles and yet they are going fast I know that. When I get to the edge of the cliff I take the path down to the beech. Sometimes the tide is in and sometimes it is out. If its in I pick my way over the rocks until I find a good one that I can sit on and gaze out to sea, its my kind of meditation it is the way I have of going into a kind of trance like a medieval monk or nun. I don't know if I believe in God but if I do its the God I find when I see the beauty around me and when I can hear a sort of silence even though I can hear the sea lapping on the beach. Lapping is a funny word for what the sea does a dog laps in great slurps and a cat laps in fast little sips but the sea doesn't lap it pats the sand – not when there's a storm of course but when it is calm which is my favourite way of being by the sea. When theres a storm it is exciting and the sea chucks itself at the beach but I can't hear the silence in the same way even though I know its there. I sit until seven o'clock and then I go back up the path and fill the kettle and put it onto boil and I wake Gray up so we can sit outside the tent and drink our tea. There are still not very many people around so its like having the grass and the sky to ourselves and the persons who are around are like ourselves sort of quiet not shouting greetings or anything but just a morning and that's it, not asking questions about what we're going to do that day, or talking about the weather. After we have had our tea we go and have showers. By this time more people are coming out of their tents and theres a kind of slow bustling about as they get their cookers going and the smell of bacon frying does me in. I am always trying to lose weight and I try not to have a fried breakfast but I can't not on a campsite. Gray cooks the breakfast I watch the bacon going that funny reddish brown and all the fat coming off it and I try to get him to throw the fat away but he says that's the best bit and he makes fried bread and crispy eggs in it. So I decide I won't have any lunch but I know I will. There will be fish and chips in Whitby or pies to take on the moors. And ice cream if we're in Whitby in the afternoon. By teatime we're starving so we have sausage and powdered potato or steak and powdered potato or something else and powdered potato. Gray does all the cooking while we're camping and that's what he likes to cook. And we go down to the beach again, even if weve spent all day there and look for things in the rock pools and its the best way to relax that I know. When the weather isn't so nice we go on the moors, there are some lovely walks and the time we go is heather time so the bees are busy and the sky larks are singing. There's silence there too. Or we go into Whitby which has lovely red-tiled roofs and little lanes leading to the harbour you can see the abbey from the harbour. I like Whitby because the lanes are crooked and because harbours are interesting theres something always going on boats coming in and people on boats doing things like washing decks or polishing brass. The dogs on the boats are funny because they have life jackets on like people. I said to Gray surely the dogs can swim and he said but if there was an accident it would be silly if the owners had to look out for their dogs when they should be looking out for themselves. But I also like Whitby because of Dracula he is weird and because of St Hild. Hild was such a great lady even though she didn't win at Whitby it showed that women could be important and have important things to say and do. She's one of the reasons I decided to come to university because she didn't become important until after she was a widow and I thought if you could do that in those days then I could something these days. The abbey is beautiful even though its in ruins some people say its spooky. Whitby has silence too. Except for the gulls there are always gulls of course but they make things silent too. Most of all I love going to Whitby because its not Leeds and its not Liverpool. I never came here until I met Gray it is another of the things he is my prince for. He loves the lakes more than Yorkshire now but I am not sure those mountains sort of topple on you, though I like the Loughrigg one that is more open and of course where the college is is very open, its flat. I hope Gray doesn't stop finding Whitby a special place for him because it will always be special for me. By Hild Whittaker."

'She may be scatty, but her description of Whitby is not bad. It's sensitive. The sea making her meditative. Being by the sea can do that.'

'Yes.'

'I'm not sure about the medieval nun, but she writes a bit like you, Miriam, "the sea patting the sand".'

I shivered. You do not write like me.

'Are you okay?'

'Cold.'

'I won't be late.' He kissed me on my forehead. I knew he was worried because the door didn't slam.

The beach of the suburb where I grew up wasn't beautiful, it was for everyday swimming, the sand coarse and gritty, the water cloudy with estuarial mud. Further out, where the river became the Atlantic, the water was cleaner.

Sometimes, no, it may only have been once – though clear in my mind – my father took me and Anna Maria along the coast to where the dunes became hillocks. We'd slipped and stumbled our way to the crests, become one with the sand, the wool of our sweaters garnering particles as we rolled down and down pretending to be young children instead of the adolescents we were. Standing up, we had shaken ourselves in a wild dance over Feo, who had tobogganed after us, his forepaws splayed. Then, his backside and his eyes clotted, he'd run around us yapping, until, bored of our inattention, he stopped to lick himself, then trotted off to sneeze at the salt water.

On the shoreline, my father made a fire of drift wood and a fisherman's net washed up by the winter storms. He beckoned to us and we ran to him, our gym shoes flapping and flopping with their load. Grains trickled down our cheeks from our hair – we had to wash it that night, a chore, both of us had thick hair which took ages to dry – as we had Meesterr Schor, as Anna Maria called him, for maths first thing, and it would have pattered onto our exercise books.

My father gave us a bucket and told us to walk out over the rocks and lift the seaweed to pick the black mussels from the crevices beneath. Feo came too. He rushed at the waves and we shouted to him, come boy, *venga*, afraid he would drown, or, trying to rescue him, we would, but he didn't obey either language. I turned and signalled to my father, pointing to Feo. My father whistled. In mid-rush, Feo whirled and darted back to bounce around the person he adored second only to my brother. Then we inched forward, balancing, steadying ourselves. At the lip of the rocky platform, squealing as the spray hit us, we plunged our arms up to our elbows, groping for the sharp shells, curling our fingers to pluck them by their roots. After twenty minutes, hands numb, arms not belonging to us, water seeping up our sleeves, we had a half bucketful, but it was enough. Wet, exhilarated, we brought our booty back and laid it on the seaweed my father had draped on the fire, not quite putting it out. The mussels steamed and opened. Scraping the meat from each with a half shell we swallowed them and their liquor until we were sated.

Hild

Ed and she went away the whole of the summer holiday – well she went to start with so I was able to go and see Ed about my courses, and then they went to America because Ed told me he was going to attend some conferences and it was a good way to get to see his son Tom. I said it must be sad for him not to have him close by – Tanya isn't very far away but we miss her, Gray misses her more than me but that's because I am so busy, but Ed was brave and said that was the way things panned out sometimes he got on with Tom very well and with Laura. When Jeff first told me to write a journal he also said it was a good thing to do as much writing as possible of all different kinds, like with reading, not to just read good books but to read anything so I thought as Ed wasn't in the country I'd practice my writing by sending him cards, and some to her too, I didn't want her thinking I was chasing Ed. In the end I wrote so many cards I just stuck them into a big envelope and stuck them in his letter box. I didn't write any cards when we went to Whitby because I didn't think it was fair on Gray to have me writing all the time.

It was great when I enrolled as a student, exciting. First there was the excitement of coming here where it was all new and then the excitement of being with new people even though most of them were much younger than me. One of them asked me how I'd come to be here why didn't I go to college in Leeds and I said I wanted a challenge, besides I hated Leeds, and this college did a foundation course in English even though most of the students did ecology or business or something like that. There were just enough of us for the foundation English course to run, in fact Jeff said I was his salvation, because I was on the course it could run. So everything was great but I didn't get to see Ed except in the canteen once or twice when he was with her because he wasn't running any of my classes. I don't know why he wants to be with her, she's so stiff.

After that there was a difficult bit it rained the whole time and Gray got really fed up and wanted to go back to Leeds and Newcastle, he tried to make me laugh by saying we'd go back east from the wild west but we couldn't, it would mean me leaving uni and anyway our tenancy was for a year and if we left before we'd have to pay for the studio and wherever else we rented. The studio was really cold and damp and it cost a fortune to heat because our landlord said we had to keep the pre-payment meter he wasn't having any tenant leaving him with a whopping gas bill. He wasn't really our landlord he's what's called a land agent, for the estate. He was posh. He came round to see us and he was wearing a tweed jacket and corduroy trousers. Gray tried to say we would never do that but he wouldn't listen and then Gray got really down and so did I because he was saying we couldn't afford to be here. It's the only bad bit of living here, it is so peaceful and friendly, but not the land agent, it's even more difficult than dealing with the council. So I went to see Ed because he's the student counsellor and he was wonderful he listened every time I went, and he sorted out our bills but even then we couldn't manage so after I'd written to Dr Farrington he found some money which meant I could go on being a student.

Jeff let me join his creative writing group it's a class he runs for students but other people can join in, and actually most of them weren't students and I loved having people to write for and reading to them. It was wonderful though Angie and Suzanne are only there because they have to be, they are not real writers, I think they are doing it as a subsidiary. She read something and Jeff made a joke about her having written about tea cosies, but the thing she read was about her being school librarian and how she tried to get the kids to read Dickens and had a row with her best friend because she talked in the library. It was in South America and the ballet teacher had bulging thighs. She didn't sound as if she liked his thighs bulging. We were doing life writing and I wrote something about me as a child which was, my dad was ... and my mum looked the other way because. I don't know why, but she did. I can't write it in my journal but it was different writing it as if I was someone else. I read it out. That was the day me and her turned up early and she said that the Virgin Mary knew what it was like to have a son murdered as if it didn't matter. It nearly made me cry. Gray says I am sensitive, too sensitive sometimes, but if he'd seen the things I've seen he wouldn't say that, even though he is my prince who rescued me from my family. He says he has seen the same things but I've never told him what I've seen so he doesn't know, but I loved my daddy. So classes were great, and friends, especially Magda and Jeff was great, he was always asking me to read my stuff, and Ed was great, so kind. He was one of my saviours I call them. People who turn up just when I need them and help me. Sometimes they are women but mostly they're men. I thought she might be one but she's always behaves as if I'm not really important to her. I don't know who is important to her, except her kids she's got two both at uni, one in Sheffield and one in Warwick, she told me that. It was the day I began to feel that I was really getting to know her. But it didn't last. She went back to being sort of distant immediately afterwards. I told her about Tanya's having her baby and how I was going to see it and I'd bring some pictures when Tanya sent them through. That's when she said about Jesus being murdered it was unkind when I was so happy about Tanya and the baby to remind me of death. Especially after I tried so hard to get to know her. I'm sure she did it on purpose. It reminded me of Liverpool and Leeds. The women in our Co-op in Leeds kept a watch for women who had anything wrong with them and asked what's happened so they had a chance to say if they were being hit. Gray has never hit me. Well only once. Ed enjoyed getting little notes and texts from me telling him how much I enjoyed being at uni and how wonderful the campus was, so pretty in the autumn with the red leaves he said they were maple trees like in the States it reminded him of the States, as well as English oak trees, and so I sent her messages too and rang her up to tell her about books I was reading and how fantastic my start in uni had been thanks to her and how much I admired her, and how kind she was as well as Ed. Gray said wasn't I overdoing it a bit especially as I nearly ran out of minutes on our phone and texts, but I said she needed to be appreciated. He said she had a very hard hand shake was she a bit aggressive and I said I thought she was a bit lonely. She didn't seem to be able to make friends how I could so I was making sure she knew that I liked her as well as I did Magda, even if she found Jeff difficult. She's quite friendly with Nicole I've seen them together in the canteen sometimes when Nicole has to come to this campus, usually she is on the other one.

Runaway

And then you ran away.

After finishing the day in a state of gloom over another report from Francesca regarding finances, Ed returned for dinner with the Vice-Chancellor, who was doing his twice yearly tour of the constituent colleges of the university. As Ed's partner, I was invited, but the university's formal occasions made me impatient. The student body representatives summoned to drinks, the speeches from the upper echelons of the hierarchy, spoke to me of an exclusive society to which I did not want to belong. Even Ed's promise of the catering school's pheasant didn't tempt me. Plus, I was writing hard and I seized the opportunity to continue.

Eventually I closed my laptop and went into the living room. I hadn't drawn the curtains or switched on the lamps. The moon was high and full. Because there was nothing to warm its light, it gave the room an intense stillness. For comfort I wrapped myself in a velvet evening cape stolen from a university flat mate, the hood up over my head, and sat on the sofa looking out of the window. A thick hoar frost glittered on the grass. I caught sight of Ed leaving the main building. Through the horizontal limbs of the cedar, I saw the catering students as they slid down the drive to the main road where the coach waited to take them back to Carlisle. Their shouts reached me, distant but clear.

Ed came across the lawn. Behind him he left huge footprints, black against the frost. The sight of them had an odd pathos. I forgot the financial restrictions which imposed added roles on his already heavy work load. Forgot his awkward arms and legs and remembered his passion for the Lake District and some of the oldest mountains in the world. Forgot his sometimes infuriating objectivity and remembered his absolute love for Tom. His love for me.

Ed closed the front door.

'You okay?'

'Yes.'

I'd put the malt on the table. He poured himself a shot and came to sit with me.

'Good look, the cape.' He turned my head to him so he could kiss me. The hood fell over both our faces and it was dark, the malt smoky on his breath.

Then he pushed the hood back.

'You have wonderful cheek bones, don't hide them.'

I kissed him again. 'How did the evening go?'

He swallowed some more of his drink. 'Better than I expected.'

'Who was there?'

'The usual. And Hild.'

'Did you talk to her?'

'A quick word. Or rather she talked at me, you know how she does. She was serving canapés. She said she liked being involved. Also it made her extra cash. I asked her how things were going.'

'And?'

'She seemed to think now she'd been to see Liam she'd be able to concentrate on her courses. I recommended giving up Jeff's workshop, if she was under pressure.'

I said nothing.

'She said it wasn't an issue, it was part of what she did to relax. She was in good form. You know how she can look– '

'Unkempt.'

'A bit harsh – though she was a tad scruffy. I put it down to the bug she's had. Graham rang earlier in the week to explain why she was absent. But she was upbeat.'

'As she is when she's enjoying herself.'

'Yes. Pretty too.'

'Dinner good?'

'Food wasn't bad. You should have come. The Vice-Chancellor's talk wasn't over-long.'

'No, I'm only an occasional – '

'Doesn't make any difference– '

'And I don't suppose there were many other partners.'

'A few. Not many.' He stroked my hair. His smile was bashful. 'I want to see you in the moonlight, all of you. Let's go to bed.'

I woke in dread. The phone was ringing. Who was it? Simon telling me something had happened to one of the children? Laura about Tom?

Ed sat on the side of the bed. He leaned down to the alarm in an attempt to see the numerals without his glasses, hissed, 'What time is it?' at me, and said, 'Hello, who is this?' into the receiver.

It was 1.23 a.m.

He listened, mouthed, 'Graham,' and yawned. My dread receded.

'Not since early evening. She was helping out at the dinner with some of the other students. Didn't she tell you?'

His yawn stopped halfway. 'You haven't seen her since you went to work?

He gestured at me and I put his glasses into his hand. He put them on and pushed them up to the bridge of his nose, unable to think without them.

'Has she done anything like this before? . . . She

hasn't got her key?'

He replaced the handset in its cradle. 'Hell. Hild's gone missing and hasn't left a note.'

'She'll have gone to visit someone – Magda and Milosz?'

'No, Graham's tried them.'

'Another man?'

'Don't jump to conclusions, Miriam.'

'I'm not. As you said last night, Hild is very pretty sometimes – what are you doing?'

'I'm getting up. I've got to go round and see him.'

'Why?'

'Because this is not good news for the university.'

'Why?'

'Students doing silly things is never good news. Besides he's in a flap. Get dressed, Miriam.'

'Why me?'

'Because I'm asking you.'

'Wouldn't it be better if I stayed here – in case she tried to reach you?'

'No, it would be better if you came. I'll leave a note on the front door saying where we've gone. Be responsible, Miriam, you've tutored her. You're one of the people she knows best.'

I was one of the people with whom you first had contact, not one of the people you knew best.

Unwillingly, I got out of bed. The room was cold. I put on one, then a second, thermal top, followed by a sweater, a gilet. I pulled on leggings, trousers, knee-length socks. From the cupboard by the front door I hauled out my boots and my coat, pulled my hat down to my eyebrows, put on my gloves. Any empathy I had for you after reading your Whitby piece, already damaged by Ed comparing you with me, was eroding.

Ed waited, dressed in roll-neck, tweed jacket, scarf and gloves – his typical winter outfit. He had a sheet of paper in his hand. He went ahead of me down the stairs and I punched the override on the thermostat. I wanted it warm when I got back.

At the entrance to the block I found him searching the path.

'What are you doing?'

'Dropped the drawing pin.'

'Stick the note in the jamb and shut the door.'

Instead of retracing his dark prints to the drive, Ed went across The Close and took the lane running past the allotments and the churchyard. It was the quicker route into town, and discreet. In summer it was full of tall, frothy white flowers and something like a large forget-me-not. Now the gravel, frostbitten, crackled under our feet.

The parking area at the back of the Co-op was full of the vans of local firms. Swainton and Formby, Griffiths and Allardyce, Brown and Son. Graham's van, Wentworth's Bakers, was there as well. Ed began to sprint, skidded and returned to a walk.

Coming into the empty high street was like entering an old-fashioned picture book, flaking window frames and chewing gum bespattered pavements disguised by the moon's light. The street door was open. Even though there was only a lock-up underneath, Ed and I tiptoed on the bare stairs. The door to the flat was also open. Knocking, Ed went in. Magda and Milosz were looking at Graham, who sat, dressed, on the sofa bed, staring at the floor. The duvet was rumpled. Had he just got out of it, or had the bed been unmade for the past twenty-four hours?

He had a cigarette between his fingers. He lit it and inhaled mechanically.

The bright cushions you'd told me about were flattened, and the bunch of artificial flowers you got from the garden centre, not quite big enough to fill its vase, had slipped to one side. I saw the grease on the hob. The flat wasn't clean and tidy like you said. The table had a plate and knife and a mug on it. The plate was covered with crumbs, the knife smeared with butter or margarine. Milosz and Magda were still huddled into their parkas and wore their fur hats. It seemed colder in here than outside.

'Should we put the heating on?'

Graham carried on staring at the floor as if I hadn't spoken.

'Do you know how to do it?' Ed asked.

We were talking over Graham as if he wasn't there, or was incapable.

'There's the fire. It's on the meter. It's run out.'

Milosz and Magda's hands felt around in their pockets for change. Ed put his hands in his pockets. They emerged, empty. I put my hands into mine, but I knew there would be nothing there. All I had brought was my keys and my mobile.

I looked at Milosz. He spread his palms upwards. He and Magda had no cash either. 'We will go and get some from my house. It is a few minutes to go there.'

They made a lot more noise than Ed and I did. Being familiar with the place I supposed it didn't strike them they might need to be quiet. As students, the fact the university's reputation might be compromised by your going missing wouldn't occur to them. It wouldn't have occurred to me. Not immediately.

Ed sat down at the table, pushing the plate to one side.

'So you haven't seen Hild since you left to go to work

yesterday morning, Graham?'

'No.'

'Were you expecting to see her at all?'

'No. she was serving on at college like you said. She was gone by the time I got back, so I had a bit of tea, watched a film, then the fire went out. I went to put some money in meter, but there wasn't any.' He waved his hand in the direction of a small cup on the mantelpiece.

'I thought Hild would bring some, from tonight. So I wrapped the duvet round me and started watching another film. About one I got a bit anxious, like. She goes to see them,' he indicated where Magda and Milosz had stood, 'sometimes, though not so late. I didn't know what to do. I didn't want to set off by ringing the police. I rang Magda and she said what about I ring you.'

His explanation was toneless. He looked around for somewhere to stub his cigarette. I passed him the plate. He went back to staring at the floor unaware of Ed's scrutiny.

'Any clue where she might have gone?'

He shook his head.

'What was she wearing? Was she wearing a coat?'

'Reckon so.'

'Gloves, scarf, hat?'

Graham looked at Ed, looked at the pegs by the door, and repeated, 'Reckon so.'

Even through my layers I felt chilled. You had less clothing, and the assumption had to be you were somewhere outdoors, exposed to greater cold. Unless, despite Ed's protest, you were with someone else. Man. Or woman.

'Why might Hild have gone off, Graham?'

Ed waved a finger. Warning me. Too personal. It was a repeat of the picnic. The wrong thing to ask. And Graham's reply was so unguarded I wished I hadn't.

'She had a row with Tanya. About the baby. She had a bad do at Whitby.'

Ed prompted, 'Also, she's been ill.'

'She wasn't ill. She was down. Said she couldn't face being in classes, couldn't think straight, so she got me to ring up and say she was sick.'

'She was fine when I saw her last evening. Said everything was back on track.'

'She's always good when she's at college.' He was echoing what I'd said earlier.

There were footsteps on the stairs, Magda and Milosz with money for the meter, but Milosz came in by himself.

'I have told to Magda to go to bed.' He closed the door and fed coins into the slot of the black box behind it, 'She is preg-nant.'

'Fantastic.' It was – a fantastic time for such an announcement, the opposite of Graham's misery.

Milosz turned round. Ed gave him a brief smile of congratulation. Graham didn't seem to have heard.

'It is fan-tas-tic – it will be twins. She is getting big already.'

He crossed to the fire and lit the gas, went to the cooker, checked to see how much water there was in the kettle, filled it, and put it on the ring.

'What is it we do, Dr Gallagher?'

Ed checked his watch. 'It's half-past two. Tea would be good, then a search of the area – the main street, the estate, the churchyard, the allotments, and the grounds. If we don't find her, the best thing is to call the police.'

'She won't be in with the graves.'

'Why not?'

'It was what started things at Whitby, them and the Dracula outfit.'

'But Miriam read me the story Hild wrote about Whitby. It showed a deep love of Whitby, and Robin Hood's Bay. Going to camp there.'

'She does love both of them, but 'til now she's only ever been in summer . . . She was in a funny mood from what happened in Leeds. We went up on the cliff three times, the third time was after we'd been to the Dracula Experience, there was a moon and then there was fog and she thought it was creepy.'

You said one of the reasons you liked Whitby was because it was different to anywhere else, Dracula made the place different, made it weird.

Milosz poured out mugs of tea and tipped in sugar.

'Milosz and I will search. You stay here with Graham.' Ed took his mug to the sink and dribbled in some cold water. Milosz did the same. They gulped their tea down and replaced their gloves. 'It's ten to three. We'll search until four, and then come back. Call us if she returns.'

As they were leaving, Graham lifted his head and looked at them helplessly. Like a dog whose owner has died.

I didn't want to stay, he made me feel guilty, but after a few minutes I forced myself to crouch at his side.

'Why don't you come to the fire? You must be cold.'

He got up from the bed. The backs of his shoes were trodden down and he shuffled them towards the table. He took out a cigarette.

'I don't smoke indoors. Not usually.'

'I know.'

'Because of her asthma.'

'Yes . . . Graham, do you think you should tell someone what happened? In Whitby I mean. It might help the university.'

'Hild admires you, you know. You're educated, she's

always going on about how strong you are, how she wants to be like you.'

Graham was wrong. In the last few weeks I had felt less and less strong, and except for brief interludes, more and more unsure of myself. I didn't know what you wanted, when you said that, but you didn't admire me.

'I'm not strong. She'd know if she knew me better.'

'She thinks you are and it's what she thinks, not what she knows, what matters. I reckon it's why she's run away tonight.'

'Because of me?'

'Because of everything. It was supposed to be something new, but it's not turning out the way she wants. She reckons she can get the education, but she can't get . . .' He stretched behind him and picked up a notebook, putting it on the table in front of me.

'I found it the other day. She left it open.'

He stubbed out his cigarette and lit another.

'Read it, it tells you.'

'I can't, Graham.' I pushed it back.

'"I want what she's got" is what she wrote.'

He looked at the journal with longing. It was how you had looked at the photo of my parents, but where your look was covetous, Graham's was one of love. I was sweating. I unwound my scarf from my neck and placed it over the back of my chair.

'What did happen in Whitby, Graham?'

'It started in Leeds really. We went to see Tanya and Liam.' He stopped talking, flapped his hand, a motion of despair.

'She said at Jeff's, Dr Young's, workshop that you were going. Did you see Tanya's boyfriend as well?'

He stirred.

'No. Brian was at work. We were meant to be staying the night. His mum and dad were to be off visiting their other lad. He lives down Ipswich or somewhere down that way. And there'd be enough room for us. But he's a lorry driver, and he had to take a load to Spain or something, and he wasn't going to be in Ipswich, and Brian's mum and dad didn't go, so there wasn't any room. Tanya didn't say until the morning we started over and it was too late to change things, I'd booked time off.'

'It must have been disappointing, not staying.'

'It was gutting, we really looked forward to being with Tanya and the baby overnight. She met us down by the Merrion Centre where there's space for the pram in the caff. It wasn't a pram, Tanya had, it was sort of a buggy, but expensive, and Hild brought clothes for Liam, nice ones. It was going all right, he's a good baby, he was awake, but he didn't cry, looks like Tanya did when she was little. He'll be freckly, sandy-haired. Like my dad. Not like me and Hild . . . It was going all right until Hild said why couldn't we have gone to the house to meet them, and Tanya said Brian didn't think it was a good idea. I was a bit fed up but Hild was . . . she can be . . .'

He hesitated, then continued. 'I was wanting for her not to begin anything, so as things could be sorted, but she started in asking what the problem was. Tanya said, "There isn't one, or rather I don't have one, Mum, but Brian's a bit uneasy about you."

'Hild said, "Why is he uneasy about me?", in a really quiet voice, and Tanya looked a bit scared and said, "Like when I was little, Mum." Hild said, "What do you mean when you were little?" Tanya said, "I told him 'cause I thought it was funny." Hild sort of, she sort of went inwards, and said, "Told him what, Tanya?" I said, "Now everyone keep calm," and Tanya said, "Some of those daft things, like the time we ran away to the airport when I was little, and when we went to London and you bought tickets for lots of shows–"'

His monotone didn't do justice to the explosive scene.

'She's gone before?'

Ed had asked the question when he was motioning for his glasses. Maybe Graham didn't answer, hadn't told him this was not the only occasion.

'First time was when Tanya was about four. We had a row, Tanya doesn't remember, but she does the rest. She used to go off, take Tanya. Anywhere. To sort of pretend it didn't happen, wasn't real, make it a bit of fun, she used to call them her breakouts. Like a day out. But it was always at night. The last time was when Tanya was thirteen. Tanya wouldn't go after that.'

His cigarette had burnt right to the filter. He flipped it onto the plate and sat there holding the empty packet so loosely I expected it to fall from his hands.

'Hild . . .'

'Was she angry?'

I should have been feeling for you, but I wasn't. In part I felt an awful kind of glee, in part vindicated. I knew there was something wrong about you.

'Yes. Especially angry when Tanya said Brian was worried about the story of Hild's little sister being dangled over the lip of the bridge above the Mersey by Hild's dad.'

'What a terrible thing to do.'

'If it happened – sometimes she makes things up. Might have been something she read or seen on the news. Takes what happens and makes it her story. She was . . . Later she said she was mortified. She said we'd to go, right away, and leave Tanya to her snotty boyfriend, who thought she wasn't good enough for his baby son, like she'd ever do anything to hurt him, like she'd ever done anything to harm Tanya . . . Tanya cried and said, "don't be like that Mum", and I said "try and get Brian to see things different – we could call in on the way back". Tanya said she'd try and I said I'd ring from Whitby. Hild was standing at the caff's door looking as if she'd leave on her own if I didn't go, and if I didn't what would happen then, so I had to.'

His voice became clearer. 'This row's been coming.'

'Why do you say that?'

'You've got kids. Hild was pleased when you moaned about your kids not getting in touch. Made her feel Tanya not telling us about the baby to begin with was all right, was the kind of thing kids do when they're growing up.'

I remembered complaining about my children. It was one of the remarks I'd made as a sop to you, a remark to allow me to escape from you. Discomfited, I overfilled the kettle, poured some water out, put it on the ring, and asked, 'Do you want more tea, Graham?'

He didn't move, didn't answer.

'It was going to be a bit of fun, Whitby, a treat for being a nan and granddad. I thought it would be good, with it being Hallowe'en. I forgot about the amount of people there would be. 'Cos of Leeds it was afternoon before we got there, and the place I'd booked didn't have a room for that night. They sent us to a house down the street which had the one to spare, fourth floor. Hild spent most of the night going backwards and forwards to the window– '

His mobile rang. He turned away from me and said, 'Yes, that's me, Graham Whittaker.'

Not Milosz. Not Ed.

'Is she all right? . . . Carlisle? . . . I'll be there soon as I can.'

Still turned away, he said, 'It's police. Motorway patrol. They've picked her up. They reckon she's okay. They're taking her to the Infirmary because of the cold. They said to meet them there.'

I didn't ask him why you'd been on the motorway. I turned off the fire and the gas under the kettle. Graham put on his coat. The cuffs were frayed and dirty. I wrapped my scarf around my neck and went down the stairs, leaving him to lock up.

Outside, he looked at the pavement, then out of the corner of his eyes at me. 'Do we have to tell about the police?'

'I can't think why anyone should need to know.'

'Can you ask Milosz and Magda not to say?'

'Yes, when I phone Milosz to tell him to stop the search.'

I rang him first so he could go home to Magda. I relayed Graham's request. As I knew he would, he replied with his customary, 'No problem'. Then I rang Ed, who wasn't happy the police had found you. Like Graham, but from a different standpoint, he wanted no one else to know.

I walked back to our flat angry. I was angry because I would have liked to delight in the black immobility of the graves in the churchyard and I wasn't able to do so after all that had happened tonight. I was angry because in my mind the image of you walking down a deserted M6, your hair glowing down your back like phosphor, might have been comical, but it was too strange, and my sense of humour had gone. I was angry because I felt as if somehow you'd made it my fault you had run away, and your "breakout", the action which had given Graham such heartache and exposed him to humiliation twice in one week, was a stunt to get yourself noticed. I was angry with Ed because he had inveigled me into teaching you, and I was angry with myself for giving in. I was angry at my lack of generosity. Because I was angry with myself I was even angrier with you.

Then it was all over campus. You had a bad time with your daughter who refused to let you see her baby. So you'd run away. I didn't understand how the Leeds fiasco, embroidered in the retelling, had got out. It couldn't have come from Graham. Magda and Milosz had promised to say nothing and – I thought it unwise – Ed insisted we say nothing too.

The story had to have come from you – you must have told someone. In the summer I heard you describe where you lived to Magda and Milosz. The account – of never being sure if you would find Graham's work van there when you got up in the morning, of cars with doors torn open because the owner had looked at someone as they walked past, of cars raced across what you called the Rec, then torched, of police helicopters with search lights circling over the estate every night – was offhand, flippant even, but it didn't hide the reality. If it was real. Graham said you made things up.

You'd done the same thing over your argument with Tanya. Graham said you were mortified at Brian's knowing about your escapades, and I think you'd tried to soften his rejection by turning it into an amusing incident. Now I was less angry and was thinking more clearly, I imagined you must have been heartbroken. If this was how you communicated the news, your listeners would have understood the real story. I squirmed for you.

The following day there was an item about you in the *Cumberland and Westmorland Herald*. It said you had been found wandering along the motorway's hard shoulder, singing. It was just a short paragraph, but you were the one person who could have given the paper this information.

Depending on the perspective, whether student or

staff, the detail – the singing – created a picture of you as either unconventional or unbalanced. From the university's point of view, the editorial, which queried the rigour of their student entry requirements, was worse than the earlier radio report and worse than the item itself. It was too much for Francesca. On the Monday after your discharge from the Infirmary she rang Ed early, summoning him to a conference she had managed to organise with you during the weekend.

'Why does Francesca want you there, Ed? Why not Jeff?'

'She wants me there as the co-ordinator of the "buddy" scheme.'

'The buddy scheme? The scheme Francesca had you set up in the summer?'

'Yes.'

'But don't you think Jeff might want some say in this? After all he is director of her major course – and her academic mentor.'

'It's a pastoral matter.'

'Good luck . . .'

When he had gone, I looked at the newspaper tossed on the floor by Ed's desk. It was folded to the article and your photo was uppermost. It took me by surprise, as had the one of myself I'd found amongst our father's things after he died, but for the opposite reason. Maybe the photo of you in the paper surprised me not because, as I had first thought, you were anonymous and lacked definition, but because, looking at it again, you were chameleon. Changing your 'you' according to your whim.

On the day of my father's funeral in Santiago, Teresa had arranged for his and my mother's photograph albums to be got out. In the photo taken by the pool I had glimpsed me and recognised then I was not able to change my 'me'.

Will and I never discussed why he refused to come to the funeral. His excuse, not leaving his cattle because they were in the middle of calving, was unbelievable and hurtful. We didn't write for sometime, and when we went back to exchanging monthly letters other news took precedence and I never gave him an account of it. Now, looking at the photo of the chameleon you, who had so dislocated me, I needed to tell him what happened. He was the only person who really knew me, the only person who might understand why 'me' had imposed such unthought exile on myself. I opened my email and began a letter to him.

. . . as you know our father took everything important to Chile. His blues and tango records – you were so cross with him about them – the photographs. When the call announcing his death came through, everything became a rush. I rang you in Santa Rosa and managed to get hold of Simon at the office, who said it would be easier if I went on my own. He came home, strapped the kids into their car seats and drove me to Heathrow. I changed planes in Florida.

At the airport, Raoul met me in his Mercedes and drove me to Teresa's apartment. There was no tall vase filled with an expensive display of colours in the lobby. I said, 'No flowers? No birds of paradise?' and Raoul smiled gently and replied that it was perhaps because our father, his stepfather, was dead? Did I think it was a mistake?

He put me into the elevator, said he wasn't coming up, pressed the button for the sixth floor. It slid up its marble shaft, the doors opened and Teresa stood waiting. She was as brilliantly, as absurdly, elegant – still with metallic eyelids – as when we first met her, when I was twenty and you were nineteen, and Dad insisted we go and paid for our flights. I think that was the only time you visited them?

She was flourishing a cigarette holder of black polished lacquer. We kissed cheek against cheek, the usual undemanding welcome, and I felt able to tease her about still smoking. She said it was only when she couldn't go without. On the balcony, if it was fine. If not in the guest bathroom with the extractor fan on like Paloma (the maid, you never met her).

Then we went to sit in the lounge, the flamboyant canopy – the one with huge red peonies the same colour as her fingernails (do you remember it?) – shading the glass wall. I asked '¿Cómo murió?' Teresa said it was a heart attack, in the early morning. He got up from the bed called our mother's name, her name and 'y cayó en la cama . . .'

The funeral was arranged for eleven the next day. Led by the funeral director with a brass-topped cane, Teresa and I walked to the church behind the hearse, along with Teresa's three sons, their wives and a number of the children. At the church we were greeted by members of our father's bridge club, some colleagues, and a few of those ex-pats who won't leave after retirement because they've stayed so long they regard it as home. Like the Smiths in Buenos Aires. Remember them?

The church was ornate and the coffin was draped in a silky ivory cloth. From beneath my mantilla – Dad requested all the women wear them, I cannot think why, he was never religious – I saw Teresa's eyes swing around to the coffin, and she whispered, 'It is your mother's wedding dress, the silk. Paloma unpicked it, washed and ironed it. Paloma was devoted to your father. He was always so nice to her.' Do you remember how Dad was always punctilious towards maids, secretaries and drivers?

At the start of the mass we were splashed with holy water and then censed with incense. It was all very formal and rather terrifying, and the sweetness of the incense mingled with the scent of the wreath of lilies made me feel sick. I had to swallow several times and Teresa gripped my hand in her lace glove.

It lasted an hour, then we crept through the streets in the long funeral limo, preceded by the hearse. We sped along the freeway to the cemetery – both the limo and the hearse were Mercedes and they were very fast – where the funeral director got down and walked in front of us until we reached the Ortega family plot.

It was a weird day, Will. I have never told anyone else of this, but waiting in the sun for the committal, I looked through my mantilla at the black lace covering the heads of Teresa's three daughters-in-law, and a physical shock, as if I'd touched the end of an electric plug just removed from the socket, ran from my fingers to the soles of my feet. It was my dream, the one I had the night Dad died. I dreamt I was at a graveside with three veiled women, their faces averted, but it was not Dad who was dead, it was Simon.

I woke up screaming.

Simon said, 'Shush, shush, you'll wake the kids, it's only a dream, it's your dream, it's not true', but I knew he was wrong. It wasn't only a dream. In some part of me there was a sorrow so deep it could only be felt in dreams, but I didn't know what I was grieving for: our father, our mother, my marriage – Simon's refusal to come with me was the beginning of the end of our marriage – or the exiled me.

Afterwards there was lunch – chilled fino and three courses – and the family bid me goodbye. Paloma tidied up, set the dishwasher going, and after many handshakes (she was very warm-hearted) went to catch the bus to her flat in the suburbs. Teresa went to smoke on the balcony – still wearing her patent funeral high heels – and said she'd asked

Paloma to fetch the photographs and put them in the dining room for me.

The albums looked dusty, they hadn't been opened since we went to stay with Dad and Teresa as part of our honeymoon. I don't think I told you about that either. I was ashamed. Simon didn't like South America, or our father. He didn't say so, but it was declared in the careless way he looked at the photographs, and his offhand refusal to take them to England. Dad looked rueful, and I can still feel his sadness. I realise now he was anxious about me and Simon even then.

There was an old manila folder on top containing a handful of loose photos. A few of Granny and Grandpa in Leamington. The one you took of Mum and Dad, so serious (why?), in front of the villa, and one of me, lying on the side of the swimming pool at the Polo Club, one arm dangling in the water. I was about fourteen. Funny, I'd always thought of myself as a bit round, like Anna Maria – remember her – who had such lovely dimples when she smiled, but I was slender. Did you take that photo as well?

Then Teresa came in, with two folios in her hands and wanted to know if I was taking the albums back with me, I had to have space this time – Simon had made a remark about there not being enough room in our suitcases. At the time I hoped she had not understood. Of course she had.

I asked what was in the folios. She laid them in front of me. They were the Gaucho prints I sent you – or rather Teresa and Paloma did, it was they who parcelled them up – a retirement present to Dad from his colleagues. Teresa said they would be amusing for my 'babies' to look at, but I asked her to send both the albums and the folios to you. I thought it was more important they went to your children who were total Argentinos, unlike my children who were English, especially as the photos were nearly all taken in Argentina, or Chile, or Uruguay. I would take the loose ones. I didn't want to remind her of Simon's dislike of Dad. Teresa was not cross, more bewildered. She said I was losing my history, then she enfolded me in her arms and said, 'Two husbands buried, Miriam. I understand.' I wasn't sure I understood, but now I think it was something to do with having part of me remain in South America. Still having a foothold there. You did get them didn't you, Will? I know it's a silly thing to be asking after twenty years. Maybe I should save up and try to come and visit soon . . .

Teresa was partly right. I hadn't lost my history, I had entrusted it to Will with the albums, and I couldn't bear it if he had thrown them out. Or hadn't received them. I pressed send. How long would Will take to reply? I shook myself. I would go out for an hour on my bike before dark.

I put my bike back in the store under the stairs. When I entered the flat, Ed was already watching the news. He switched off the television, came into the hall and stood looking at me while I took off my jacket and my helmet.

'Why are you staring at me?'

'I'm not. Aren't you going to ask about my meeting?'

'What meeting?'

'With Hild and Francesca.'

I took the broom out of the hall cupboard. I didn't want to discuss you.

'Was it okay?'

I started at the front door and swept the dust towards Ed.

He frowned. 'So-so. I think we've sorted things out.'

'How was Francesca?'

'She found it difficult.'

'Finally sees what she's up against?'

'Maybe.' He grimaced. 'Hild was twenty minutes late. Completely nonchalant about running away. Said it was "in her own time".'

I snorted.

'It's not funny, Miriam.'

'Perhaps not, but she has a point.'

I swept the dust into a pile by the kitchen door.

'Not as far as Francesca is concerned – she asserted the university's claim to be interested in a student's welfare when their actions were jeopardising their progress.'

'That was heavy-handed.'

'Why are you so negative nowadays?

'Can you think why?'

He pressed his lips together, a movement I recognised as gaining control of his temper. Which infuriated me. I wasn't the villain in this melodrama.

'Francesca was trying to be supportive. But it did come out as an . . . admonition.'

I went to the far side of the kitchen and began to sweep up the bits of rice and diced vegetables where they had dropped in front of the stove. As I moved towards the middle of the kitchen, I felt Ed continue to follow my movements.

'Aren't you going to say anything?'

'Why? I don't have much interest in Hild . . . All right. How did she react?'

He wasn't deterred. 'Badly. She claimed her poor start was not of her making – it was partly due to her grandson being born, a lousy flat and money problems, but mostly because she wasn't getting adequate feedback on her work. Must you do that, Miriam?'

'What?'

'Clean while I'm talking to you. Why are you cleaning

at this time of the day?'

'Been for a bike ride. Gives me energy. And the flat needs it.'

Still in the doorway of the living room, Ed stood, hands hanging down by his side. He pushed his glasses up and peered at me, his short-sightedness making him helpless

I gave in. 'All right. I'll finish the kitchen and leave the rest. What did Francesca say?'

'She had to be tactful. She can't afford to lose students. She sidestepped the feedback issue, changed to the subject of mentoring and asked her if it would help if she had a buddy.'

'The scheme which Hild refused to have anything to do with because she'd been taught by me in the summer so didn't need a buddy?'

He missed my sarcasm. Or ignored it.

'Hild said she would accept one so long as it was the right person. Someone in tune with her interests and her course. And her age. And her gender.'

'Who is?' I went back to the hall for the dustpan.

'Most of the students are too young. Practically all of them are doing environmental science or agriculture, and are male. I put you forward.'

I stopped sweeping up bits of onion and papery garlic skin from under the vegetable rack.

'What? After what happened last summer?'

I hadn't told Ed of the effect you had on me this autumn, but I stared at him in disbelief.

'I couldn't think of anyone else who fit the bill.'

'And I fit the bill? What did Hild say?'

'She . . .' His hand dismissed words he didn't want me to hear. 'All right, Miriam, you needn't worry– '

'I'm not worrying, I'm not doing it.'

I started brushing the debris into the dustpan.

'Francesca vetoed you because you are not employed by the university at the moment. And I don't think she wanted go down the route we went in the spring.'

'Quite right too.' I emptied the dustpan with a bang into the bin. 'So who is going to be her buddy?'

'I'm to be her mentor.'

'Did you propose it, or Francesca?'

He looked at me cautiously. Since our row in the summer he had been wary of my temper.

'I did.'

'You must be . . . you've enough to do as it is, and she'll drive you . . . but that's for you to find out. How did she view your proposal?'

'She's quite pleased. Someone's got to do it. On the plus side,' he offered, 'I've been taken off the student's Christmas party committee. Francesca wants you on instead.'

'Me? But as Francesca pointed out I'm not on payroll at the moment.'

'Agreed. However as you said yourself over the Vice-Chancellor's dinner you are an occasional member of staff and as such you qualify, and you might enjoy it–'

'I don't have the time.'

'It keeps you in contact with the university.'

My voice rose. 'Like teaching Hild did?'

Ed said hastily. 'This is different. You might find it fun.'

Ed

I think you can, you must, help anyone who needs your help. It is partly why I am an educator – to help those who need help. No one helped me, my mother couldn't, she didn't have the education, and my father had gone so there was no help there, but my teachers didn't want me to leave at sixteen to do an apprenticeship, they said I should do A levels and my mother consented.

Hild needed help. It was why I supported Francesca's suggestion that Miriam run the skills class for her in the summer, though Jeff was initially dubious. We thought it would give her a good start, I never dreamt Miriam and she would be at loggerheads.

I don't know what happened. Hild was thrilled to bits when Francesca let her take the class and then she didn't turn up. Then Miriam. I don't know why Miriam behaved as she did. She seemed antagonistic from the start, when Hild was – okay she was getting things wrong – forgetting the time and failing to turn up, which annoyed me a bit, and I was slightly concerned, but Miriam took it personally, as if Hild was doing it on purpose. Then she thought Hild was after me or I was after her, which was ridiculous. I told her I wasn't in the slightest bit interested in Hild and asked why Hild would be interested in me when she had her husband Graham, who was a very nice man and very supportive of her.

I think the problem was the writing. It was okay when Miriam had plenty of students to occupy her and it was something she did in her spare time. But as we, as the university, were only able to offer the class to fewer and fewer students, to those who really needed it, like Magda and Milosz, and as she could do it with less preparation, the writing seemed to be an obsession. Her time became unbalanced.

In the past year and a half, I was running to keep up with myself, even to the point, sometimes, where I was reading university documents in bed – which Miriam said was ludicrous – but the situation wasn't helped by her mind being forever on her writing, even when I was off. It interfered with our time together. She was either scribbling or thinking about it. I could tell. She'd get a vacant look. I made a remark about it one day, and she over-reacted, demanded to know how did I think she felt at my being so consumed by the university's affairs.

I felt guilty. I knew I had been leaving her on her own, though I wasn't ignoring her, it was just I was so busy. It was a stupid thing to say, unfair, but when I wasn't working, I wanted to be with her, really with her. Once or twice she said she wanted to be more involved in university life. I suggested becoming the staff member of the town-campus link, but she said it wasn't the kind of involvement she meant. I asked her what she did want, and she said she wanted to be involved because of who she was herself, not because she was my partner. I tried to explain that the situation with staffing meant you had to accept anything you could get, but all she said was she would rather do without my crumbs of charity.

What with Miriam lying in bed all day, refusing to go out, worrying me so much I had to return to the flat to make sure she'd got up, and Hild being flaky, endlessly wanting help with finances and domestic problems, and then behaving with what Francesca – in an unusual outburst – called, "dumb insolence" when she absconded, by late autumn I was totally, completely, preoccupied by the two of them, to the extent it was affecting my concentration on my other work. And I couldn't make Miriam see she couldn't blame everything on Hild.

I didn't discover until after Miriam moved in how ambitious she was. Ambitious for herself. Not for her kids, though she loved them and missed them deeply, but she said they could fend for themselves. They had to. Everyone had to. I said people need help. She said, of course, but some people couldn't be helped, and I knew she was referring to Hild.

Buddy

I found Ed's appointment as your buddy disquieting. As was your insouciance. When I next saw you in the canteen were holding court. You looked elated, and your laughter came too often and was too aware of your listeners. I was apprehensive about Jeff's workshop. The prospect of having to be near you made me wonder whether I wanted to attend.

The workshop ran from three-thirty to six. We, you and I, reached Thornthwaite at three twenty-five.

Without preamble you said, 'I'll have to leave early. I'm having a counselling session with Ed at five-thirty for the next few months.'

'Mentoring, Hild.'

'Mentoring, counselling. It's the same thing.'

Angie and Suzanne came in. They eyed you with something like awe and asked what happened at Whitby. You didn't say, but told them you might extend your earlier piece and bring it to the next-but-one meeting. This wasn't the answer they were looking for but they tolerated it on account of your fame.

When Jeff came in, he asked, in a not wholly admiring fashion, 'How's the escape artist?'

You smiled with reserve. Who were you today? Serious adult? Reformed character? Woman with an important rendezvous with her future? Graham's disclosure of your magpie collecting of people's lives to embellish yours made you difficult to locate, and made me wary in your presence.

Surprised at your lack of reaction, Jeff became breezy.

'Well, girls, have you brought your photos?'

I found Jeff calling me a girl annoying, and extraordinary that Angie and Suzanne didn't seem to mind. Perhaps he was too distant from their lives and their age for it to matter. You bridled. It was curious. In no mood to play the heroine, gone also was your desire to please, your eagerness to do what other people suggested. The last few months' events – in anyone else they might have been disastrous – were, for you, steps in maturity. You had lost the girlishness.

Angie and Suzanne produced glossy photos from their folders.

Angie's had been taken at a party, everyone dressed either as rockers in black leather or as hippies with headbands and kaftans.

Whether it was innocent or not, your observation, 'There's a lot of smoke in the air,' brought a grin to Angie's face.

'It's joss sticks.'

Suzanne's submission was a castle, or turreted house, taken from a vantage point above the building.

You were quick off the mark. 'Where's that?'

Jeff was equally quick. 'Don't tell her, Suzanne. I know where it is, but for this purpose the others don't need to know. Did you take it yourself?'

'Yes.'

'It's good. What have you got, Hild?'

You looked irritated, but didn't say anything. Instead you produced as promised, though without your usual flourish, the photograph of your wedding. Your bridesmaids were in a semi-circle behind you. They and you carried posies of freesias. The scent must have surged and eddied around you. Graham and his best man stood at your right-hand side. Your glance slanted to the left.

'Plenty of scope there, Hild. What about you, Miriam?'

'I couldn't find a photo–'

'Really, Miriam?' Jeff was quizzical.

Ignoring him, Angie squinted at the printout. 'What is it?'

'– so I've brought something I found on the internet.'

I appreciated the difficulty. The fretting of the balconied stacks was so dominant, the bookcases behind them were almost invisible. The place might be a nineteenth century department store.

Suzanne picked the printout up, turned it around and said, 'It's a library.'

'I'm not writing about a library,' said Angie.

'No one is asking you to.' Suzanne smiled at her with a friend's scorn.

'I thought we were writing about our own photos,' you said.

Jeff was patient, 'You are. Use them to combine narrative and autobiography.'

He turned to me, 'It's an incredible place. Where is it, Miriam?'

'The Peabody Library. In Baltimore.'

'Who took it?

'Not sure.'

Jeff sighed. 'Right, you've got nearly two hours. Get on with it.'

While we were writing, Jeff annotated term papers. Or rather, while we weren't writing. Angie doodled snail shells on her paper before making a list. Were they names? Suzanne looked out of the window, clicking her biro in and out, until even Jeff's professional control snapped and he asked her to stop. I had time to sharpen and resharpen my pencil, inscribe question marks on my paper, and think about the Christmas party and its committee. Only you had your head down, scribbling. At three minutes to five you looked at the clock, and kept glancing at it, until at ten past you put your note book in your bag.

'I'm sorry, Jeff, I've got to go. I've a meeting with Dr Gallagher at five-thirty.'

'You don't have to come to the group at all, Hild, if it's not convenient.'

'I want to come, the workshop is great, Jeff, it's just I'm going to have to leave early for the next few weeks. I've a series of meetings with Dr Gallagher.'

Raising of a "meeting" to "a series of meetings" gave your mentoring sessions with Ed an importance I didn't think they deserved. And since when had you gone back to calling Ed "Dr Gallagher"?

'It slipped my mind. Ed did tell me. I'll make sure your work is critiqued at the start of the workshop. Send me what you've got as soon as possible.'

Watching you leave the room my eye was caught by the Della Robbias. After Jeff's derision over my "baroque" mistake I'd researched them. With my background, I should have known. They were Italian Renaissance. Italy. Ancona. Malfi's duchess. Angie's eighteenth. The carnival in Venice. The party could be masked. Most people enjoyed dressing up. Jeff was always going on about mummers' plays, he might do one with the theatre group. I'd get Ed to propose it to him. Where was there to hold a costumed, a masked, ball?

I looked up. Jeff was examining my page of question marks.

The reason you managed to write for the whole time was because what you sent round wasn't a fiction based on your wedding photograph but a description of your Hallowe'en experience. No mention of your traumatic visit with Tanya. No title. No paragraphs. It was one continuous flow of words unleashing your emotions. You told the reader where you had stayed, but most of it was about how the Abbey, the church, the Dracula Experience had affected you.

It was getting late by the time you and Graham got to Whitby and sorted out the guest house, but you insisted on going to the Abbey, saying it would be healing for you both. It was coming up for the full moon, but you were in luck, you and Graham were alone as you climbed the hundred and ninety-nine steps up the cliff, hypnotically whispering the numbers under your breath. By the time you reached the top you were lightheaded, gazing up at the sheer arches. They swung around you, once, twice, before they ceased to move. From the town below you heard the raucous tinkle of the crowds of goths moving between pub and pub, but you were separated from them. You were at, no you were, the centre of the great holiness of that place.

In the guest house you did not sleep. You did not want to sleep, for fear you would lose the feeling that the universe embraced and surrounded you. You left the bed to look out of the window and down the four flights of the fire escape. Never had you seen anything as beautiful as the way the latticed iron lay there stark black in the flood of light waiting for your tread. Then there was a passage which startled me . . .

"A step scarlet enticing the rise is purple it calls to me come stand on me and then on to the one above stand here, here where I can fall off leap off, it calls to me my feet tingle to stand on the first step, on the second to perch on the edge of the second, on the edge of the dance the edge of the performance of my life I want to be there to leap in scissor bounds off the step across the grey expanse of the floor."

It contradicted what I wrote in "*Biblioteca*". My paralysis when my teacher told me to dance. It represented a readiness to embrace the life you started by coming to university. I wanted to be moved but I was disturbed by your mania – because that was what I read it as, a mania born from your obsessive desire for recognition.

In the morning you were more than lightheaded, you were almost delirious. You refused any food but drank copious quantities of black coffee, something you normally hated. You were fizzing, and talked of how you understood what mystics must feel, you talked of your future, how you would get your degree, and would start a new career, though you weren't sure of the direction. You talked and talked. Graham listened.

The day was brilliant, the last day of the Celtic summer, Samhain. You knew about it because you'd studied it in Jeff's folklore module. Once more, you climbed the steps to the Abbey. This time you chanted the numbers as you went up, your breathing made easy by your joy, and were warmed by the smiles which greeted your gleeful one hundred and ninety-nine from a couple waiting to descend. You went past the Abbey, to look out at a glittering sea. The openness intoxicated you further, but also quieted you. For the first time since breakfast you fell silent. Gray and you walked along the cliffs until a sharp wind blew up, and Gray suggested going back into Whitby. You didn't want to, not yet, so you made your way back to the parish church.

Inside, you didn't talk. You read the information, walked around, examined the plaques commemorating those who had died. You were learning things, educating yourself. Your excitement returned. You looked at the curious pillars, touched them, 'It's like being on a boat,' you whispered to

Graham.

He whispered back, 'Yes, like the ferry to the Isle of Wight.' You stroked his neck, because you were so happy. Even if he wasn't clever, he could make you laugh. He took your hand and kissed the palm with gratitude. You were astonished. Where had he learnt to do that? You determined you would do more with him. You would be able to, now you were no longer conflicted over what you should or would be. You knew what you were going to do, you didn't need to be a part of student life, you had no need to fit in, you would get an education. You'd seen Tanya, you had done what you could, and she could come to see you. It was a pity about the argument, but it was over, and it wasn't your baby, it was her baby, you didn't have to worry about him.

Despite Graham saying, 'Don't, what if someone came in?' you climbed into the pulpit. At the top, under the canopy, you leaned on the ledge and gazed over the pews. You wondered what it was like to preach from, to know the soul of a town. The vicar had to be puzzled by the people brought to this town – and this building – only because of Bram Stoker. You'd never read *Dracula.* Graham reckoned he had. You said it was probably a kids' edition, but he said it was great, full of action, heroes, love. Maybe you would read it, not for the course, but you could rejoin the book club, bring it up with them, they wanted ideas for out of the ordinary novels. You'd offer to lead a discussion, it would be good for you.

On and on it ran. This was the second time you had exposed not just your grammar, but yourself, to the workshop. What was it that permitted you to do this, that didn't restrain you?

Graham sat in a pew and stared up at you. You knew you were looking good. When you felt alive like this your eyes were blue. Blue like the little flower, the speedwell, Nicole told you the name in the summer. As well as Gray and Tanya, you'd a whole new family at college. You were so, so lucky. Leaning over the pulpit you said, softly, because, although there was no one in the church, you didn't want to spoil its atmosphere of prayer, its peace, 'Why don't we go get some lunch, Gray, then go to the Dracula place.'

Gray was surprised, and you knew why. Before, when you had looked at the pictures outside the Dracula Experience, you'd always refused to go in, feeling it would close in on you, and you hated being trapped. He asked if you were sure. You came down the steps and round to the front of the pulpit and said you were happy, more than happy, with the idea. He was so pleased he proposed going to a pub, but you wanted something more significant. You decided to go to a restaurant. There, you decided what you needed was a glass, or three, of sparkling wine. The fizzing of your excitement mixed with the fizzing of the wine to make you lightheaded again. As you left the restaurant you tried to launch yourself from the harbour wall saying 'I can fly', and Gray had to grab you to stop you going over.

You reached the Dracula Experience half an hour before it closed. The girl said you were the last two ticketed entries. Up on the cliff the Abbey was gaunt. The sight of it made you shiver and you wondered if you did want to go in. You asked Graham if it wouldn't spoil the book for him, but he said of course not, it was a bit of a laugh. It was only a book anyway. You knew you and he would never agree on "only a book", but you remembered him kissing the palm of your hand and said nothing, you didn't want to spoil the day.

As you were buying your tickets, a drunk came in. The attendant told him the experience was about to close.

You quoted him, "'Fucking 'ell, that's fucking crap,

them over there they're going in, why not me–'"

He was a Geordie, like Gray, but Gray would never behave like him. Gray was steady.

The girl was unflustered. She said he couldn't go in because he was intoxicated, you and Graham weren't.

Graham was watchful but calm. You never liked drunks when you were working in the pub, but there was always someone else there to handle them. You wanted to get as far from him as possible, you reached for Graham's hand, and pulled him in to the start. The cloth over the entrance fell behind you and it was pitch black.

Your story ended abruptly, dramatically, leaving me wanting to know if the cause of your running away – if the cause wasn't me, as Graham had intimated – happened now, or later, after you had left the Dracula Experience.

'So what happened in the Dracula museum?' Angie demanded.

The vertical blinds were drawn against what was now a stormy mid-November and the overhead fluorescents drained us of colour.

'Yes, loved the writing, Hild,' Suzanne said, 'evocative, you were flying.'

'Almost literally,' Jeff said, hastening to dispel any emotion.

'It's not a museum. It's a kind of ghost ride. It was totally dark. Scary.'

'But, being brave, you clutched Gray's hand, went in and produced an interesting bit of work to boot?' I thought Jeff's determination to keep hysteria at bay was patronising, but you disregarded it.

'Not very brave, but yes, we went round, then we came back to college. We drove through the night,' you finished in triumph.

Angie and Suzanne clapped their hands.

I calculated the time it would take, leaving at about six in the evening, to get from Whitby to here. Not all night. Not unless you had left rather later – and Graham had talked about going to the Abbey three times. The third time, when he said it was foggy, must have taken place after the Dracula Experience.

'Well, you at least have written something. And Suzanne and Angie have produced some work too. What happened to you, Miriam, the Peabody?'

'I love libraries. At one time I wanted to have one, but– '

'You wanted to be a librarian, Miriam? I bet you'd be a good one.' Angie said.

'I didn't want to be a librarian. I wanted to have my own library.'

'It must be really satisfying to be a librarian.' You smiled at me.

'The trouble was, Miriam?' Jeff wasn't naturally patient.

'My trouble was I love books, but I have nothing to say about libraries– '

'Mirrie's story about her school library, Angie,' you murmured, 'you and Suzanne weren't here that day, it showed her being a librarian, putting books back, telling people to be quiet.'

'Well, I don't know what you intend to do about it, Miriam, but it isn't worth coming to the group if you aren't going to write. Would you find it easier if you took a break?'

He had done it for me, given me a way out. Now I didn't have to make the decision, could leave without disappointing Ed.

'I think a break is what I need, but I did– '

'Are you trying to be a bit too intellectual, Mirrie? Ought you to write about all the foods and the plants and things when you were young in South America.'

Angie and Suzanne murmured agreement, South America was interesting. Had they missed the undercurrent of you calling me "Mirrie", thought it amusing as they had done before?

'I was just about to say – I have done something like that. A continuation of the library story – it's about tarantulas.'

'Is it scary?' Suzanne's eyes glinted.

'Not unless you're frightened of them. Are you?'

'No idea. Never seen one.'

'I brought a picture.' I put it on the table and ran my finger across it. 'Hairy all over. Even the legs.'

'Did you bring the story?' Suzanne asked.

'Yes.'

'We haven't enough– '

Angie interrupted Jeff, 'Me and Suzanne would like to hear it.' I'd underestimated her.

'Yes, go on, Miriam.'

. . . after her clash with Nina in the library, Anna Maria had come up to Miriam and said did she want to come to tea with her. When Anna Maria's mother came to collect her she asked Miriam why she wasn't expected home. Miriam said that her mother didn't come from her room until sundown.

At this, Anna Maria's mother nodded and said, 'Okay, I will drive you home after merienda. Get in girls.'

They clambered into the back of the shabby red Mini whose cracked seats scratched their bare thighs. They zipped along the rambla towards the centre of the city, and branched off to the right through cross-hatched streets where Miriam had never been. It was the embassy quarter, Anna Maria's mother explained. Her husband was economic attaché in the Spanish Embassy. The houses were older than Miriam's, tall and thin, with long green shutters on the windows. The doors were taller and thinner too, made of wood, not fancy metal and glass. There were no gardens to be seen, or garages, or balconies above the garages.

Anna Maria's mother parked the car outside their house. The front wheel went up onto the high curb and bounced down.

'Mama', Anna Maria said, and giggled.

'Ai-ai, it is good your father didn't see that.'

'Especially if you will need a new tyre. Come, Miriam, let us go to my room until Mama has made the merienda.'

They placed their bags by the telephone table and walked through the hall. The wide wooden floor boards sloped to the outside wall, and the staircase did too. The stairs were polished. There was a smell of lavender, like the English soap Miriam's mother used.

'If you want to wash your hands before we eat, it is there.' Anna Maria indicated the door at the top of this first flight of stairs.

Miriam turned the speckled porcelain handle. Inside was the biggest bathroom she had ever seen. In one corner on its own platform crouched the lavatory. On the wall opposite there was a basin, and next to it on four paws stood the bath. She climbed the steps and sat on the lavatory. From there she could see the soft grey fluff of dust beneath the bath. A bit of darker fluff moved. She froze. The darker fluff stilled and she stood up, not taking her eyes off it. She shook out the pleats of her skirt. Reaching behind her, she waved her hand about until she found the chain. She pulled it. At the rattle and rush of water the darker fluff scuttled to the wall behind the bath. Spider. Tarantula. Miriam didn't much mind them, but she kept out of their way. She came down from the platform, moved softly to the basin, her eyes on the floor, and ran cold water over the tips of her fingers. It would have to do. She shook off the drops of water and backed to the door, keeping watch on the floorboards.

Outside, Miriam turned to go to Anna Maria's room, but at that moment her mother called, 'Venga a la mesa,' and Anna Maria bounced out and ran down the stairs, jumping from the last two with a thud. She swung around the banister and skidded into the dining room on the left.

'Ai, Anna Maria,' her mother semi-scolded.

On the table there was a kettle of hot water, three cups and saucers, a jar of Nescafé, a tin of condensed milk, and a plate heaped with churros slick with oil. They seated themselves.

Anna Maria's mother handed them a paper napkin each and offered Miriam the plate of churros.

'Cuidado, estan caliente.'

They were so hot the fat in the churros crackled as they dunked them in the coffee. Between them they ate the plateful.

'Gracias, Mama.'

'Gracias, Señora de la Torre.'

'De nada'.

They returned upstairs, licking their fingers. Anna Maria's room was long and narrow, and dim, although the shutters were open. Through the window Miriam saw the garden: a lawn, clumps of bamboo, and in the centre a mass of pointed crimson and orange flowers which shrieked at the sky with brilliant blue tongues.

'They look like enamelled herons about to fly from their nest.'

Anna Maria shrugged, indifferent, 'I shall show you

my collection. See.'

She switched on the light, the shade limiting the feeble yellow glow to the centre of the room. She pointed under the table at four or five large jam jars. At the bottom of each one Miriam could just see a dark shadow.

'Tarantulas.'

'From under the bath?'

Anna Maria laughed. 'Sí. I will give them their merienda now.'

'What do you feed them on?'

'Mice. They are in this box.'

'Are they alive?'

'Of course. Do you want to help?'

'I'd rather read.'

'There are magazines.' Anna Maria indicated the neat pile on the straw-bottomed chair beside her bed. She bent down, lifted a jar on to the table and started to unscrew the lid. The tarantula scrabbled ineffectually at the glass sides. Miriam ignored the magazines and scanned the shelf above Anna Maria's bed. *Green Mansions*. One of the girls' favourites, it was always out of the library. She hadn't read it. Maybe Anna Maria would lend it to her . . .

I finished.

'They're horrible.' You shivered. Another thing which frightened you.

'I like your life, Miriam,' Suzanne says, 'Hild's right, the food's luscious.'

'It would be useful if you did what we agreed,' Jeff said.

'Hild didn't. Doesn't.'

Jeff gave me the look which told me you were a special case. I didn't think he was far wrong.

'It must be weird having a maid. Did it make you lazy?' Your eyes had changed. They were like the time I met you in the Co-op, round as marbles, not blue any longer. They must lose colour when you are thwarted. Challenged.

Angie looked at you disapprovingly, 'We weren't talking about maids and au pairs, Hild. I agree with Suze, your life's really interesting. See you around, Miriam. Come back soon.'

I got up. For the first time since term had started I felt at ease. I was released from the obligation to come to Jeff's class which Ed made me feel, freed from having to meet you. Yet there were parallels between you and me. You were offered the chance to leave the workshop if it interfered with your mentoring. Then I was offered the chance. You didn't accept, but I did.

If I thought you phoning me was maddening, your return to phoning Ed drove me crazy. Meeting with him each Monday – everything always happened on a Monday as if there was a build up to a crisis over the weekend – gave you the idea you could ring him incessantly – two or three times an evening, sometimes as late as midnight, and, as soon as it might be accounted permissible, as early as half-past six in the morning.

'It's only me,' you said. 'It's only me. Can I speak to Ed, please?'

One evening I screamed, 'I know it's only you.'

I shouldn't have, and it was a mistake, but it wasn't just me who was suffering, Ed was too. Often I held the handset to my chest, whispered your name, urged him not to take the call, but he would make a face and reach for it. While you talked he looked at the television, the sound turned down, or resumed marking a student's assignment. Sometimes he soothed or coaxed, and I knew you were weeping down the phone. Sometimes he was congratulatory. 'Great, Hild, great.' Then, 'Great, Hild,' and I knew you had received a good grade, or were lit up with a new idea. Whatever he said, even when he was being enthusiastic, his voice was restrained. I was puzzled you didn't notice, didn't hear it. In your place I would have done. When I argued with him about you, saying you needed professional help, not a student mentor, he said he had suggested it and you had said no, he was as good as any professional. One day you rang up Francesca and told her how wonderful Ed was.

The evening after I shrieked at you, Ed was out.

The phone rang. As soon as you heard my voice you cancelled the call. I knew it was you because I keyed in number recall. Five minutes later the phone rang. I didn't answer it. I was sure it would be you. The phone fell silent. I keyed in number recall. It was you. Another five minutes during which I tried to read. The phone rang again. I didn't answer. I checked. It was you. And again, and again, again, again, again, again, again, again, again, again, again, again, again. Each time the phone rang I checked, and found it was you. Ten times in the space of an hour and a half. At the eleventh time I was beside myself. I wanted to pick up the phone and howl at you, but I knew you would put the receiver down and I would be doubly frustrated.

When the phone ceased to ring I called my daughter, my son, a friend in Surrey. Everyone was out. I put the handset back on its cradle, and immediately the phone rang. It rang for a long time. When it stopped I checked the number. This one was local, with an area code, not a mobile, not your mobile. I knew Jeff's office number, Ed's office number, the university number, the Library number. These were the calls we made to landlines.

It was you, I knew it was. You had gone to the

lone telephone box in town, the one at the bottom of the drive leading to the campus, maintained for the sake of the students. You were trying to trick me into thinking it wasn't you so I would answer the phone. I looked at the time. It was a few minutes past nine. I'd go and see what the number in the telephone box was.

The full moon and the frost at the start of the month had been followed by the persistent rain we'd had in the early autumn, and the lawns had returned to their sponginess, but tonight it wasn't raining and the air smelled of damp and mushrooms.

I wondered if you would be there at the telephone box, ringing and ringing, ready to greet me with frenzied laughter. To my disappointment you weren't. I knew you would deny everything, but I wanted to confront you. I wanted to hit you.

The street lamp beside the box wasn't working. I opened the door, but the light didn't come on. I was sure there ought to be a light. Every telephone box had one. Even though I knew it was useless I leant forward, straining to see the number, then let the door creak shut. I was looking for the number of a phone, used by an unknown caller, in the dark of a cobwebbed telephone box which hadn't been visited in months. Your instability was triggering insanity in me. I knew what I needed. I needed company, but not Ed's. I saw him too much and we talked too repeatedly about the same things. His work, his work, his work. My work. Recently, you, you, and you.

I stood there, considering. I could go and see someone in the other staff flats, but I'd never done it before and I didn't want to start speculation over what was happening in ours. I didn't want anyone knowing there might be something wrong. For a moment I was frightened. I could think of no one to go and see. There was no one I could drop in on at around nine-thirty at night. It didn't happen in England. Not in my life, at least.

Magda and Milosz. They were accustomed to people dropping in. Maybe I could go and see them, but I needed an excuse. During my latest bike ride I had discovered a barn which I thought was an exciting place to hold a student Christmas party. That was sufficient. I would go and discuss the party, and the barn, with Magda and Milosz.

I walked down the yard to their entrance as the clock on the church tower was striking ten. Was ten too late, now Magda was pregnant? Before I could press the bell, or run away, there was the the clattering of feet on the stairs and the door opened. A man was silhouetted in the hall light. He was somewhat surprised to see me, but instead of asking me who I was he stuck a skinny cigarette in his mouth and lit it. Then I recognised him. It was Milosz's friend from the picnic, Chris Juste. He recognised me too. I could hear music playing.

'How're you doing?'

'Fine. Are Magda and Milosz in?'

'Yup. I came down for a smoke – otherwise I have to lean out of the window.'

He shouted up the stairs. 'Hey, Magda, Milosz, it's your friend . . . ?'

'Miriam.'

'Miriam.'

Milosz called, 'You are welcome Miriam, it is a pleasure.'

He greeted me at the top of the stairs, 'Enter,' led me to where Magda was seated and turned off the music.

Magda patted a place beside her on the bed they used as a divan during the day, 'Sit.' She leaned back against the scarlet and black bolsters.

'What would you like, a beer? Magda is having Romanian tea.'

'What's Romanian tea, Magda?'

'Rose petal, very nice, very good for you.'

'That would be lovely.'

Chris came in bringing with him the warm scent of rolling tobacco.

'Give them up, Chris,' Milosz said, 'so you do not have to run up and down the stairs. It is not good for your throat. Chris is here for two nights to do a gig. In Carlisle.'

'It's midweek so they take unknowns.' Chris's smile was self-deprecating, and winning.

'We are going to hear him tomorrow. Do you want to come?'

'It's bit short notice. Another time let me know, and I'll see if Ed would like to go.'

'You can come without Ed. There is one more place in our car.'

I was tempted, but a vision of you with students half your age made me refuse.

'Next time.'

Milosz handed me a cup of the palest pink steam, then, holding bottles of beer, he and Chris settled onto harder cushions on the floor.

'So what is making the pleasure of having you, Miriam?' Milosz enquired.

'Were you having a late walk? It is good for making you sleep.' Magda asked kindly, and I wondered at the source of her wisdom.

'Ed's at a meeting. I've had this thought about the Union's Christmas party – I've come to try it out on you.'

Their faces awaited my idea.

'What about a masked ball – like the carnival in

Venice?'

They said nothing.

'I know the carnival happens in February, but masked balls took place at lots of different times – New Year, May. December the thirteenth. The party is on the twelfth.'

'You've researched this very thoroughly, Miriam.'

I couldn't tell whether Chris was being complimentary, but Magda smiled at him and said, with apparent seriousness, 'You could do a cabaret, Chris – dressed up.'

'I saw this barn the other day – not in a very good state, but not derelict.'

'And quite nosy?'

This time Magda defended me. 'Miriam is not so nosy, Chris.'

'I was biking past – it's easy to stop and look in. It's got a platform, a raised threshing floor which would make a stage for the bands.'

'What's a threshing floor?' Chris was riffling through a handful of CDs.

I'd had to ask Ed what the platform was for, but Chris's question galvanised Milosz. 'A threshing floor is where you beat the corn to separate it from the–?' He looked at me for help.

'Chaff. What do you know about threshing floors, Milosz?'

'My family for ages was having a farm. I know what it is to thresh.'

Chris stopped his riffling, 'What about electrics?'

'Will it not be a lot of work? Is it not too late to set up?' Milosz asked.

'Not if I took the plan to the committee this week. The Union always organise tickets and publicity, it would just be a bit more focussed this time. I'm sure the catering students would find it interesting to cook for.'

'Like the dinner they do for the Vice-Chancellor the night Hild goes missing? Pheasant, tough, and potatoes, greasy. '

'Milosz.' Magda dragged out his name in reproof.

'Goes missing? Who's Hild who went missing?'

Had Chris not been informed of this scandal in the life of the campus?

'I didn't know you were at the dinner, Milosz? You didn't tell us when we were looking for her.'

Milosz said, 'I was plating up in the kitchen,' and to Chris, 'Hild. The one at the picnic. She was found by the police. She walk up the M6 singing to the moonlight.'

'How . . .'

'Unusual.' I finished Chris's remark for him. I didn't want to discuss the subject of your aberration. It reminded me of my own.

He went on, 'What was she singing? *Blue Moon*?' Did his question contain a trace of ridicule?

'Chris?' Magda didn't understand his reference.

'It's an old, old song.' I tried to explain. 'I think a moon's blue if there are two of them in the same month.' I realised this didn't make anything any clearer. Nor did it deflect Chris.

'The one at the picnic. She the woman who didn't like the thunder?'

'How did you guess? It is her.' Since being dragged out on the search for you, Milosz had been less supportive. It was Magda who offered you friendship.

Were they more normal than I had been when I was a student? Maybe the demands of getting a job after graduating meant they had to keep any irrationality within the circle of their peers and their family, whereas you had broadcast yours to all and sundry. As, if I didn't get back soon, I would. I hadn't left a note to say where I'd gone and Ed might be ringing round any minute, like Graham had done.

'It will take two hundred. It's on a lane off the Penrith road.'

'To take two hundred is big enough for a ball, Miriam?' Now it was Magda who was doubtful.

'Not everyone will be up for it. At least I don't think so.'

'Why not?' Chris's question was unconcerned, but it threw me. In my imagining I saw a large crowd of people dressed fantastically, dancing to an insistent hypnotic beat in a space glowing with colour. On the other hand I had counted on a manageable take-up.

'Why do you not suggest it to Ed, Miriam? If he is comfortable with it, you can take it to the Student Union.'

'Magda – your English gets better and better – comfortable – like an armchair or a bed.' The edges of Milosz's eyes wrinkled with pride.

Chris started examining the CDs, keen to get back to the music. 'I reckon it's a goer.'

'And it would be good fun.' Milosz seemed to be coming round.

'It is the longest night in the old calendar,' Magda said.

'How do you know?' Chris asked.

I looked at my watch. It was eleven. I had to leave.

'My grandmother used the old calendar. It was a time of mischief. Foolishness.'

'What?' She'd got Chris's attention.

It seemed Magda's grandmother's life was steeped in ancient ritual. When I left they were discussing what Magda called the Feast of Fools. As the door closed behind me I heard Magda say,

'I understand now what Miriam is meaning, the blue moon, it is the double moon, the betrayer moon.'

Feeling my way in the dark over the slate flags of the yard, it occurred to me. Just as I couldn't think who to visit, Ed wouldn't have known who to ring. The only actual friend – apart from Magda and Milosz – I had in the university, and she was Ed's friend first, was Nicole, who lived in Carlisle.

Hild

Tanya didn't want me having anything to do with her baby. Or it was Brian didn't. He said I must have been a bad mother. He didn't say it he wasn't there, but that was what he meant when he said he was worried. I'd brought such great things for the baby, done extra shifts at the pub when I should have been studying, I knew I had to work harder after seeing Tanya to make up for them because I hadn't got behind but I hadn't exactly done the work properly. I was angry. It wasn't fair him saying that. I wasn't a bad mum, it was just I wanted something more than being Gray's wife and being Tanya's mum. I saw it in my own mum and dad, she didn't do anything if he said no. Gray was my prince and I would never give up on him but we didn't like the same things. He just liked being at home. He should have been the mother I said and I should have gone back to my job straight after Tanya was born. It was just shop assistant but I could have got promotion. And the Co-op looks after their workers. Though we both liked Whitby. When he was working on the beer lorries we'd go by train, he'd put the tent on his back and we'd take the bus to the camp site, or if it was just a weekend we'd borrow a van from a mate, so long as we got it back first thing Monday morning no one noticed and we always filled it up. I just had to get out sometimes and I took Tanya so she'd know a mum could do things as well as a dad. I called them my breakouts, kind of a joke so she'd know we were going back. So she'd know it wasn't for real, I wasn't really leaving. Once or twice I asked the police to give us a lift home, I said we'd lost our bus money. Tanya asked if it was a lie, and I said not really, we didn't have any bus money with us. We'd come out free. We'd go and walk all over at night. The night's very important to me, it's when I know I'm different and can do things, be things, be unusual, be someone.

When Tanya said that I felt like crying but I wasn't going to, not in front of her, as she'd tell Brian I cried. Gray was trying to calm things down like he always does when me and Tanya get into it, and I said he was to come with me or else I'd go off on my own. I love Tanya, but me and her don't always agree and she'd sided with Brian. He's only eighteen and she's only seventeen what do they know about it. Anyway we went to Whitby but it was all spoilt and when we got there we couldn't get into the guest house because we hadn't booked, and Gray had done overtime to get the money for a little celebration and I was so sad for him because it was all spoilt, Tanya and Brian had spoilt it for him. I stayed awake all the night and looked out, the roofs were all shining grey in the moonlight it was nearly a full moon, it was so beautiful I made a resolution. A new year's resolution because in the folklore course Jeff said, it was Samhain, the end of the summer and the Celtic new year. And here I was in Whitby where Hild was a saint and she was a Celtic saint, my patron saint I said once to Gray who didn't understand, he wasn't brought up with saints like I was. I would get an education, I would get a good job, I wouldn't let Tanya and Brian get to me, it wasn't my baby.

The next morning we went up to the Abbey again, we've been loads of times before but it was extra special this time because I'd made up my mind, I was going to be someone and I knew it would happen. After we'd been in the Abbey we had a look in the church and I felt brave and clever and when Gray suggested a proper dinner I suggested the Dracula thing. He kissed my hand I didn't know he knew how to do that. So we had a proper dinner in a restaurant down by the harbour and it was great I knew I could be whatever I wanted to be, I just had to set my mind to it and it would happen. I even tried to fly! I said look Gray I can fly! and he grabbed me and said not to be so silly, but he wasn't cross, he never is, just sort of admiring that I could be so different from all the girls he knew before me, all the women in our block in Leeds. Magda said he was the saint. I said he was far too interested in me to be a saint and she giggled. Then we went to the Dracula thing and it was scary, too dark for me and there was this drunk, but I held onto Gray and made it out all right. The next day was lovely too we went up on the cliffs again and had dinner out and then I said to Gray let's go up to the old graves next to the abbey and see them at night before we go back. We set off and it was all right we got to the top and got to the graves which were as if they'd grown, there as if they'd got feet. I found one which had the date of death as the same day as my birthday. Then Gray said look at that, he sounded really quiet and really surprised. I looked up and there was this fog rolling over and over up the cliff as if it was an animal and was coming to suffocate us. I screamed it's alive, and Gray said don't be silly, it's a harr, but he'd never seen one so thick. It kept on rolling towards us and then it was over us and I couldn't see Gray and I couldn't see the cliff edge. All I could see was the date of death of this person which was the same day as my birthday and I wondered if that would mean I would die on my next birthday. I cried where are you, Gray and he said, stand still don't move I'll come to you. It seemed to take him ages to come to me but he did and by then the fog had got onto my chest, I was heaving, and I was too frightened to move. He said we'll go down, but I was too scared to move, I didn't know which way was down. Look he said, if you look you can just see the outlines of the graves and if we go through them we'll get to the steps. We did get down, I was holding on to his hand and crying but it took us longer than we thought and then we had to drive all night because Gray had deliveries the next day. He had to deliver over to Cockermouth and Whitehaven. I was worried he'd fall asleep but he didn't he just kept on driving.

When I got back I remembered about Tanya and I felt really depressed, like I used to after my breakouts. Gray rang the uni for me to say I was sick, but I wasn't I was just really down. In the end he said I'd got to back to uni otherwise I'd get kicked out. I said they don't kick people out of the uni and he said maybe not but you enjoy it. I said I used to. He said try it one more time and he made me go to do the Vice–Chancellor's dinner because I'd already said I'd wait on. I saw Ed there and he was really caring and it made me feel so much better seeing him and being with the others I wanted to stay out. The moon was completely full that night so you could see the mountains far away. I got a lift to Carlisle in the student coach, but then I didn't know the way back so I got myself dropped off at Junction 44 and walked down the M6 because I knew how to get back from there. My heart was soaring and I sang. I always sing when I know I am going to succeed. And I thought I bet Miriam could never do something like this, she's held back by her degrees it's made her stiff and proper, my degree won't hold me back. I am a born free child, and it will be the first step in going forward.

Then there was a fuss because the police picked me up and took me to the hospital and there'd been a big fight so I had to wait in Casualty and while I was waiting this reporter turned up asking about the fight and one of the police said you want interview her, she's a student, she's just been picked up walking down the M6, singing and she's clean. She wrote it up for the paper and Dr Farrington was not pleased. But like most things that happen to me it turned out well. And if it hadn't been for Tanya I wouldn't have got depressed and Gray wouldn't have forced me up to the campus he'd have just said if you don't feel like it don't go and then I wouldn't have got Ed as my buddy.

He's a counsellor. He is my saviour. I thought he might be and he is. He listens to me so I feel I can tell him everything about what it is like to be a mature student in uni and how I got here, and the things which are holding me back. He is so encouraging, he doesn't mind when I ring him, he just looks after me so well. Ed suggested her, Miriam, at first, but Dr Farrington didn't want that. I told Dr Farrington, I rang her up and said the best thing she could have done was make Ed my buddy in the buddy scheme, he was such a lovely man, and she laughed and said she'd tell him I said so. Gray said he thought I was a bit in love with him I was ringing him up so often, but I said Ed didn't mind, he understood. He said to make sure I didn't ring him so much it seemed like stalking him, and what did Miriam think. Her I said, I've told her he's one of my saviours and Gray didn't say anything.

Ball

I didn't care whether taking on the staff role on the Christmas party committee would help to maintain my standing with the university, but it developed my connection with the students. I began to get to know them from a different perspective. They had a mixture of youthful optimism and, studying practical subjects, directness and sense, which made working with them enjoyable.

The Students' Union adopted the concept of a masked ball with enthusiasm. With equal speed they vetoed the customary offer of the Sports Hall – free – as a venue. It wasn't what they envisaged for an alternative event. The difficulty was there was nowhere suitable they could afford – until I told them about the barn. They decided it was what they wanted.

It wasn't what the administration wanted, but the Union officers went all out to win over Francesca. By taking the event beyond the campus, substituting a hired-in hog roast for the food usually provided by the catering department, using local bands instead of a DJ from Carlisle, and engaging the town's taxis to ferry the partygoers to and from the venue, they demonstrated the potential for involving the local community and putting money its way. This was a plus with the university which always sought to enhance its profile with the public.

At the same time, so as not to burden the finances of their constituency – the formality of their language in their dealings with Francesca entertained me – they would have to sort out costumes as well as tickets, and they set out to prove they could keep costs down. The bands would come for little more than fame and beer. The bar would pay for the hog roast. They had it sorted. Francesca – I couldn't tell from Ed's report if she was reluctant – acquiesced.

Having found the place, I got the job of negotiating with the owner, who said she thought combining town and gown excellent and was agreeable to the students using it, especially as in the spring she was turning it into a space for the equestrian business she was setting up. There was not much harm they could do to her property except burn it down.

Misguidedly, I relayed her comment to Ed, who relayed it to Francesca, whose reservations surfaced. She said the university would take responsibility for the insurance. The Union was relieved as the additional premium had come in at far more than they were expecting. That is, they were relieved until Francesca stipulated there would be no naked flames inside the building. The generators for the bands and the hog roast would unquestionably be outside, but there were to be no candles, and the braziers they wanted in the yard would be proscribed if there was a high wind.

I was in Reception talking to Nicole, who'd come across from Carlisle to do mid-year reviews, when the deputation to change Francesca's mind left. As student entrepreneurs they had dressed well for the meeting, the girls with full make-up, but she wasn't persuaded. They came over and complained to me. I said bargaining with Francesca was their province and I hadn't the authority to reverse her decision. Besides, I reminded them, the university was taking on the insurance.

However, I had better news. In return for using her barn, all the owner wanted was a modest donation to an animal charity.

'Which I find amusing. The last time I was there a deer carcass was dripping blood over – what do they call those outhouses next to them, Nicole?'

'Shippons.'

' – all over the floor of the shippon.'

They didn't quite see the incongruity, but went off discussing the date for a site clean-up.

'And she's going to provide straw bales for seating,' I called after them.

'They're charming, even when their plans are stopped,' Nicole said to me. 'Lunch?'

On our way to the canteen, Nicole said, 'Ed tells me you want a full-time post.'

'I am having second thoughts. Being involved with this ball stops me working.'

'What are you working on?'

Nicole knew I was – I didn't call myself a writer – writing, but I didn't want to talk about it.

'A sort of memoir.'

'And you're not?'

'Not enough. I'll be pleased when I can focus . . .'

She looked at me as she had Hild after the thunderstorm. 'On something? Anything?'

I changed the subject. 'What was Laura like, Nicole?'

'Why do you ask?'

'Isn't it normal to wonder about an ex-wife? And everyone – sometimes I feel they sort of mourn her?'

'Only because they knew her.'

'Did you?'

'Enough. She was her own woman. She didn't like this place – too small, too claustrophobic. I wouldn't want to live here myself. Anyway, it's you Ed's with, not Laura. How are you going to decorate the barn?'

Her question put a stop to intimacy.

'We are going there on Saturday so Ed can do preliminary health and safety. I might get some ideas then – it depends on what the art students come up with.'

'How is health and safety Ed's job?'

'It's not, but he offered. Francesca doesn't trust me.'

My reply must have been a bit sharp, because Nicole threw me another questioning look, as if she wondered about my relationship with the university.

When Ed saw the barn he said, 'Does this woman really suppose she can turn it into a holiday centre?'

He walked across to a cobwebbed window and pressed his nose to it.

'What sort of capital is it going to require?'

I followed him. 'Not a holiday centre – an equestrian centre.'

A terracotta jug filled with seed heads sat on a paint-spattered table. Ed continued staring in.

'Ed, stop it, she lives here.'

'She does?'

'I told you. She's an artist.'

'I thought you said she was a riding instructor.'

'She's that as well. This is the back. Come round to the front.'

The front was better. The dry stone wall which surrounded the yard had been repaired, and the gate and its hinges were new.

'See – things are being done.'

Ed grunted. He had supported the idea of holding the party here, but now he was anxious because it wasn't taking place on campus and felt it would be extra work for the staff. It was a conservatism I hadn't noticed before and it surprised me.

I went up to the farmhouse and banged on the door knocker.

'Look, Ed, a green man.'

The knocker waggled its tongue lewdly at me. Ed glowered as if it was a real man.

No one came to the door. I was disappointed. The owner was so different from the campus staff I wanted Ed to meet her.

'She must be off somewhere.'

Ed stood with his back to a clump of nettles and inspected the building.

'It's been re-roofed. Let's have a look inside.' He walked back to the great door and pushed at a small one cut into it. It was very low and we had to bend down to enter. Inside, the gloom was lit by holes where the walls met the roof.

'What are the holes for?'

'Owls,' Ed said. He ranged across the space examining the floor, his bad temper gone.

'It's a bit uneven. They'll have to take care not to trip when they're dancing.'

'Should we say something on the poster?'

'No. It's not too bad – a barn dance is after all a dance in a barn.'

'It's not supposed to be a barn dance. It's supposed to be a masked ball.'

'Yes – but it's not going to be eighteenth century music, is it?' He swung himself on to the threshing platform. 'It'll be a bit difficult getting the bands' gear this high, but not impossible.'

'They'll manage. Do you think the art students ought to have a different brief? So the guests have an idea of what to expect?'

'Maybe.'

'Something less Venetian, more rural?'

'It's your show, Miriam. Drop them an email when you get home. Let's take a wander over to Ullswater. There's time to get to the top of Gowbarrow before the sun goes.'

We had been a couple of times to Aira Force but had never made it up the fell. When we arrived, the car park was already in twilight, deserted, but as we left the stream and the woods and emerged into the open, the sun lit the bracken, turning it a dark copper. Saucers of frost remained where its rays hadn't reached.

'Which way?'

'We came–' Ed stopped. He went on, 'We won't go round by Yew Crag, it's too long. Straight up the middle.'

I set off. I felt light-hearted. The afternoon was making up for the last few months of Ed working all the time. I didn't want to be tied to him, but I'd missed doing things with him.

The grassy path zigzagged effortlessly up and over one long slide of rock to a pointless cairn at the top. Ed pushed back a couple of stones which had become dislodged, and we looked down to the lake below. There was no ripple on its surface, not even a steamer moving. It was still, perfect.

Then Ed said, 'The sun'll have gone in an hour. It's not worth going any further. Let's head home.'

As I started back across the turf I caught a glimpse of something moving below me. My shadow. Ed's was there too.

'Look, Ed. It's separate from me.'

I danced. My shadow capered, its legs frolicking. Or rather I started to dance and it followed suit. It was liberating not being attached to my shadow, yet unnerving. I controlled it, but it had a life of its own. It was mine, but not mine.

'It's a sort of Brocken spectre.' Ed semaphored. His shadow followed suit. 'You get them on mountains – usually where there's mist or snow.'

'My brockenspectre? It's a good luck sign.'

'It's to do with how the light is refracted and strikes the contour of the land. The complete ones have haloes.'

I bowed. It bowed. My shadow put its arms out to Ed.

Next thing I was on my back, sharp-angled stalks imprinting their design on my buttocks, the bracken sodden beneath me.

My email to the art students, proposing they dream up something more bucolic, resulted in posters which had ticket prices and information concealed in dripping, foliage beards, and hidden in cat-like ears. From the mouths lolled tongues, urging the readers to make their own masks, create their own costumes, go wild. It was as if the farmhouse door knocker had manifested itself in the students' minds and fingers. The Union put the posters up in dozens on both campuses and the tickets sold too well, making Ed more anxious. I heard Francesca's voice through his anxiety. He and other senior members of staff were summoned to meet with her.

'How did the council of war go?'

'All right.'

'That's non-committal – what did you decide?'

'We are going to alert the police to the possibility of trouble from outside. And Francesca's going to pay the site staff double time to act as bouncers.'

'Seems decisive to me.'

'This is your fault, Miriam, you know.' He said it

lightly, but he wasn't joking.

'Why is it my fault?'

'It was your idea. What on earth made you think of it?'

'I was watching Hild at Jeff's workshop and looking at the Della Robbias.'

'What's Hild got to do with it?'

I didn't answer. The two ideas, masks and Italy, had come together. I understood the treachery of *The Duchess of Malfi* and the deformity which masks hide. I understood their association with you.

'You can't hold Hild responsible for everything, Miriam.'

'How is she?'

He avoided my eyes. 'She's in the mummer's play.'

'What part has she got?'

'I don't know. No one will know who is playing whom.'

He spoke as if it was none of my business.

'They're going to be completely covered,' and on safer ground, now he was talking about something factual, he relaxed, 'Jeff's found some pictures showing mummers with rags coming down from the crowns of their heads.'

'They'll have to leave a gap for their eyes.'

'No, you can peer through. Jeff says it's why they were able to get up to all kinds of things in the past.'

'What kind of things?'

'Going after people, making sexual advances in public.'

'Oh.'

'What do you mean, "oh"?'

'People haven't changed. Make them anonymous and they'll do all sorts.'

He looked sceptical.

'Wait here. I'll show you my outfit for the ball.'

I went and dug out the gaucho clothes I had unearthed from the trunk I kept under the stairs along with my bike. I stepped into the trousers, wound my crimson belt around my waist and pulled on the brown poncho.

'What do you think?'

'Won't they make you a bit obvious?'

'I'll be masked.'

After the initial rush, sales dropped and the fuss over the tickets died down. Everything went well until, with five days to go to the ball, the hog roast went bankrupt. Ed told the students to arrange a barbecue. They dismissed his suggestion.

They wanted the evening to be authentic, not a barbecue and bands do. They'd get the catering school to do provide a cold banquet. It would be better for the vegetarians.

'The whole thing's taking up too much of everyone's time and energy.'

'It's not your time and energy being taken up. The students have shown initiative. Stop fretting.'

I expected the campus to be in an uproar for the forty-eight hours before the ball, but the setting up was carried out with efficiency. Through the bursar, Francesca had directed the ancillary staff to help the committee. The caretakers enjoyed the alteration to their normal day-to-day existence. They helped clean the barn, manhandle bales of straw, hump bags of charcoal and braziers, cart bundles of holly and ivy, and quantities of bay. Because the agricultural students, given the task of felling the row of conifers running along one of the boundaries, managed also to chainsaw two magnificent bay trees. Instead of finding the students' action funny, as he might have before he was so overworked, Ed was outraged. I could see why, they'd taken some growing, but their mistake was opportune and I commandeered the branches to decorate the stage.

The electrical equipment arrived on time. The decorations were delivered from the Art School. Nicole had unearthed a cache of saris, hidden in Textiles for at least ten years. She appropriated them, and slashed them into bunting without conscience. The owner lent us an enormous ladder. I was thankful Ed wasn't there when I watched the students taking it in turns to balance on the top rungs as they hammered portraits of the green man to the rafters, half hiding them in the leaves of the foliage. I noticed Nicole absented herself while they were perched so high.

She returned bringing news of the menu. It was to be based on the medieval practice of piling food on tranches of bread.

The bread would satisfy, while heat would be created by strong herbs and warming spices. There would be rice fritters with cumin and cardamom, potato cakes enriched with horseradish, bean rissoles spiked with green chilli, pickled pink peppercorns in the coleslaw, cold roast ham embedded with crushed black pepper, roasted salmon smeared with wasabi, red chilli in the cold chocolate mousse, fruit loaf, loaded with allspice, cinnamon, cloves, nutmeg to go with the Wensleydale cheese. In addition there were going to be open pies filled with vegetables in custards flavoured with white pepper, and mince pies enlivened with ginger. These last would be heated in a couple of industrial microwaves along with the jugs of spiced ale.

'It sounds complicated.'

'It sounds delicious, and yet', Nicole's laugh was gleeful, 'hot sweet beer is a deceptive drink.'

For a second I was, like Ed, afraid of something going very wrong, but I was able to tell him, truthfully, everything was under control.

Because of your involvement with the mummers you were silent. You did not bother with me at all, but that didn't deflect my intention. I already knew how the novel would end. Violently.

In your wedding photo your eyes looked aslant from the camera, as if you were absent from the event, yet your new husband Graham and his best man had open faces, at ease with themselves despite their formal suits. Your smile was solemn, doubtful. What had turned you into the woman I knew? The woman who had altered Gray into the sad man he was today. Was it the education you sought? Had you left Gray out of your life? Or was it that you always needed recognition and married life didn't grant it. Very soon after my own marriage I wanted to regain the 'me' I had been before. Did I leave Simon out of my life because I too wanted to be recognised?

I got the box file, and three notes you'd recently sent Ed which I filched from his pile on the dining table. I hadn't looked at them, but now I decided I had the right.

"Dear Ed, I'm sorry I threw a wobbly last week, it was so silly of me, but when you couldn't see me, cancelling our meeting, I lost all confidence. Hild."

"Dear Dr Gallagher, This is just to thank you for all that you – and not forgetting Miriam– have done for me. You have been so supportive. Best wishes Hild Whittaker."

"Dear Ed, I think I may call you this after so many weeks of unofficial and official counselling, despite my being so formal in my last communication!! I just want to say that you are a very, human person, very caring, though maybe you are a bit ostrich like. Regards to Miriam.

Hild."

For a minute they shook my resolve. Maybe you were not dishonest, not manipulative.

Then I wondered why you said Ed was an ostrich. It was code, like the Cinderella story you'd written me nine months back. I had assumed you wanted to let me know of your appalling background. Now the story appeared as a warning not to get involved with a person beyond my experience, as a threat. Blinded by my role as teacher, I had misunderstood. The message to Ed insinuated he was engaged with you more deeply than he knew. It said he was too naive, or arrogant, to see what was going on. I was convinced you weren't the person you pretended to be, and I wanted revenge.

I would write the story of your wedding photograph as a dry run for the novel. I jotted down all I knew about you. Your difficult family, your work – a shop assistant in a department store before you were married, working in a chip shop after your baby was born, working in the Co-op, if indeed you had, it seemed too altruistic for you – your husband the prince, your child, your love of Whitby, the colour of your hair, the colour of your eyes, your figure, the innocent yet not innocent sexuality of your too tight clothing, your clotted Liverpool accent, your enthusiasm, your extravagance, your elation, your depression. The people you gathered round you to support you, the men who saved you and fell in love with you. It was enough to be going on with.

. . . And they are happy. The photographs show their happiness. Lots of photographs – from the window of their council flat, third floor, in one of the new blocks on the edge of the estate, of their Christmas trees, their holidays in Whitby.

He has a home, a wife. He has been granted the keys to the castle.

She says he is her prince. He has rescued her from her loneliness, from her family, from being a woman without a destiny, from other women. For despite her bridesmaids, she is never at ease with other people, especially other women. He's rescued her from her many sisters, all of whom are jealous of her, because she's the oldest, she says. Because it's what women have, they have the jealousy lobe. They're not jealous of men, because men are in charge, but women are always in competition with other women. Even when they are your younger sisters. He's found out that's why she's come to Leeds. Her family drove her to it.

He says, 'It was a bold thing for you to do.'

Heddi says, 'Not bold, just had to.'

Despite her apparent nonchalance, it was a bold thing, for she is quite timid – though she is occasionally raunchy, which delights him. She doesn't say much more but he respects her privacy. Everyone has some things they don't want to reveal to anyone.

And altogether they are happy.

They have a baby girl. More photographs. He takes lots of pictures of the baby playing on the rug, or in his wife's arms, his wife smiling at the baby. He can never capture the blueness of Heddi's eyes because she doesn't look at the camera. Her hair is longer than it used to be. All the women on their estate have long hair. It marks them out. They are the ones not working.

She doesn't smile at him much those days.

'It says in the *Post* it takes fewer muscles to smile than to frown.'

He is astonished by her shriek of rage and her tears. Didn't see them coming.

He makes her go to the doctor who gives her some antidepressants. Her and half the women in the block.

She goes back to work when the baby is two, part time in the nearby chip shop. Their neighbour looks after the baby in the day. Thursday, Friday, Saturday evenings, Greg does.

The baby grows older. She's not a baby now. The evenings Heddi isn't working she goes to classes. There is one class on writing women's lives and one on women authors, feminist ones, she says. She says the classes, they show her what has been wrong with her life. She has been too obedient. She has been a good girl. Her daughter must not be a good girl. She says she doesn't hate him, but he feels she has blanked him from her mind. He wants to shout, 'Am I invisible? Am I invisible?'

He gets desperate. One day, when she turns her face away from him as he tries to kiss her, he hits her. Once. Tentatively. He shocks himself. She looks exultant. It is her excuse. She runs away, but she can't bear to leave the little girl behind, and she comes back.

They continue to live in the same flat.

But from time to time she runs away. She takes her daughter with her.

They come back. Sometimes they are brought back by the police late at night, who say they have found them wandering along the road out to the airport. Sometimes they are brought back by the police from the centre of the city, because she has no money for the bus fare. There's always a reason why they come back.

Every time she comes back she seems less sorry. Though she says he's a good man, she says she's been unkind. He feels as if he is clinging with splayed hands and feet like a frog onto a clear plastic beach ball. It spins away from him.

Inside it two little figures spin in the opposite direction. He presses himself desperately against the ball, his lips planted on it in a kind of kiss, trying his best to become her prince again . . .

"The history of Heddi and Greg". In this fairy story, unlike in your Cinderella, there was a prince, your marriage disintegrating as you unshackled yourself from him. In reality you would never be so stupid as to let Graham go.

Like the point of view exercise, I couldn't show it to anyone. Or send it to my fellow writers. You would instantly identify the facts of Heddi and Greg's life. Your first meeting in the roadhouse on the A1 just outside Durham. It had an enormous mirror in the entrance which reflected the girl you were, with the silvery blond hair, the blue eyes, the sandals criss-crossed Greek style on your brown legs, the plump appealing lips, Graham slender, dark as a Romany, nose broken in a fight, beside you. Graham losing his job as a mechanic and having to get rid of his car. Touching up the paintwork where gravel, thrown up by the spinning wheels from his occasional rally driving, had chipped it, and selling the car to a pair of unsuspecting teachers. When you told me the story you were highly entertained at your Gray, so quiet, so dependable, being so masculine and putting one over on posh nobs. Graham following you to Leeds, getting a job as a brewery driver, persuading you to marry him. Having a baby. Being allocated a council flat, which meant, however much you hated Leeds, you were obliged to live there. The single made-up fact was his hitting you, which gave the you of the story the opportunity to detach yourself little by little, but keep him in thrall through his guilt, and his love.

I would send it to Will. Normally I was embarrassed to show him my work, sure he wasn't interested in my attempts to write, but someone had to read it.

I heard the entrance door to the flats slam. Only Ed slammed it like that. I brought up my email, put the title, *The Frog's Princess*, in the subject line, attached the document, and pressed send.

The Frog's Princess

Ed phoned from his office.

Knowing it would please him I said, 'I forgot to say last night. I have decided I'll give Jeff's workshop another go.'

He said, 'That wouldn't be' – he hesitated – 'appropriate.'

'What do you mean appropriate? You weren't happy when I left.'

'Send Francesca a copy of the story, Miriam.'

'Which story?'

'The one about a frog's princess. About two people called Heddi and Greg. The one you sent to "writers' workshop".

'I didn't. I sent it to my brother. To Will.'

'Maybe. Maybe not, but it also went to "writers".

'Oh.'

'Quite.'

His tone said I had done something very stupid.

He went on, 'Francesca wondered if sending the email was an accident.'

'Why?' I was disquieted.

'Hild's been to see her. There was a scene. She wants you sacked. Send the story, Miriam. Perhaps Francesca can wave a magic wand.'

I felt aggrieved, but in something like panic I emailed a copy of the story to Francesca. In my email I said, I hadn't wanted to create, I regretted possibly having created, a predicament for the university. I wasn't going to admit fault.

The phone went. I tensed.

'What is it?'

'What's what, Miriam?'

I relaxed. 'Nicole.'

'What have you been up to, stealing Hild's stories?'

For a moment I couldn't speak.

'You've heard.'

'Everyone heard. No one could not hear if they were in Reception.'

'Ed said Hild went to see Francesca.'

'She did, but Reception didn't get her beyond the plants which screen the visitor seats before she let rip. Or rather Graham did, as far as it's in him, with the occasional gasp from Hild when she got her breath. They had to bring Francesca to her.'

'Gasp?'

'I thought Reception might have to ring for an ambulance.'

I sat down on the floor. The window was framed by tree branches. I could be anywhere.

Nicole continued. With Gray as your mouthpiece you claimed I had distorted your life. I had made you out to be mad. I had to be sacked. I had to be blackballed.

Urged on by you – 'she kept jogging his arm, Miriam,' – Gray responded to Francesca's interjections – it was not possible to sack someone who was not an employee, Miriam Henderson was not an employee – by repeating the same accusations, making the same demands.

'And do you know what Hild repeated over and over again when she did have breath? "She's stolen my story".' Nicole paused. 'Is it true?' She was cautious, as if she didn't want to commit to one side or the other.

'No. No I haven't.'

'Because if what Hild is saying is correct,

appropriating her life could amount to the theft of her intellectual property rights.'

'I didn't. I changed it.'

'But she believes you stole it.'

'I've used some bits and altered some.'

'Okay.' Nicole didn't seem convinced.

'Anyway, they can't sack me, I'm not employed.'

'You could be blackballed.'

'What do you mean, "blackballed"? I thought blackballing a person was to keep them out of a club or some such.'

'Who is your referee, Miriam?'

'Francesca.'

'There's your answer.'

My resentment of you, smothered earlier by my near panic, surged back.

'I was doing Hild a favour, teaching her before she was enrolled. And Francesca. Doing her a favour.'

'Favours have a tendency to be regarded, and disliked, as charity. Or weakness.'

'Ed said she was frantic.'

Nicole didn't say anything.

'What am I to do?'

'I don't know.' Nicole hesitated.

Then she said, 'This is a real mess, potentially, Miriam,' and I knew she didn't want to get involved, 'see you around.'

It was a mess, but it had been created by you. My story wasn't a character assassination. All it did was show how a woman altered, how a marriage died, how being trapped could drive someone insane. In that, it was objective. If I hadn't before, I hated you now.

I got up. I hadn't done anything wrong, but I knew

you would respond, and I forced myself to look at my emails to see if there was one from you. There was, its subject "critique". I debated whether to delete without opening it. I was frightened of your tongue, worried it would be a vicious rant.

It was worse. Your tenor was measured, and all the more lethal. First you were personal. "With people like you, Mirrie, who have difficulty thinking of what to write, (I saw the question marks you wrote across your pad the day of my first counselling session with Ed), it is always easier to use another person's story."

Then you took a different angle. "Gray and I got the impression from your pieces you haven't had a very happy childhood. Not as bad as mine, Mirrie, but you were a little lonely, hadn't friends. And you're divorced from your husband, aren't you Mirrie, is that why you wrote about me and Gray as Heddi and Greg, as a disguise for *your* life?"

It was untrue, but to deny it was to admit I'd used your story.

Then your style became formal, using words I had taught you. You thought the story was quite well written, but it was too conventional to excite the reader. Had too little spontaneity. Was too cryptic.

"Cryptic" – what you meant was it left the reader with too many questions. It was the same criticism you levelled at "my mother bought a dog once". Only, as ever, you were indirect, making it difficult for me to retaliate. You were clever. First you said I didn't know what ordinary people were like, now you claimed I was conventional. Either way, I was excluded from the experience you had and your ability to capture a reader's attention.

The phone rang. I braced myself. You?

It was Ed. 'Francesca thinks you ought – no, she

insists you must – apologise, "for having caused Hild any trouble because of the seeming link between her photo and the frog's princess story".'

'I don't have to. I am not employed by the university. Remember?'

'You do, Miriam. This affair must be smoothed over, and you can't leave it to me this time.'

How had it happened? I'd helped you, and you, veering from the fawning to the hostile, stalked me, because that is the word for what you did, and had maddened me to the point where I had done something stupid. Written a story in which you were identifiable and portrayed as unbalanced. You'd capitalised on my stupidity, making sure the whole campus, if not the university, knew about it, revealing my craziness to all.

I didn't want to go the ball. Everyone would know about "The Frog's Princess" disaster, just as everyone had known when you ran away. Everyone would be talking about me.

'No they won't, Miriam. Francesca has rolled out the official secrets act. She doesn't want the episode going any further than it already has.'

'I don't want to meet her. I'm not going if Hild goes.'

'You can't stop her – she's one of the mummers, she has every right to be there. You have to attend, Miriam, otherwise people will gossip. Stop being hysterical.'

Ed was embarrassed by me. Calling me hysterical said my feelings were of no account.

'If everyone is in costume, no one will know whether I'm there or not.'

'You took on the job, you have to come. You did apologise?'

'I sent an email.'

'Copy to Francesca?'

'No.'

He was rootling through the cupboard where we kept the alcohol. Now he stopped and glared at me.

'Why not?'

'Francesca is not my boss. This is between me and Hild.'

He started pushing bottles about again. 'Where's the scotch?'

'I finished it.'

'Right, beer it is.'

He removed a can from the fridge. 'For Christ's sake Miriam, it'll be fine.'

Coming on top of his anxiety about the ball, he was knocked off balance by your reaction to what he termed my "slip-up".

'Nicole knows. She was in Reception.'

Ed pulled the ring off his beer and said nothing.

After the Christmas holiday I would look for a job outside the campus. I would commute, other people did.

To make sure I didn't go back on my decision I went to the Library to return the reference books I'd used. After I checked them in I went into Thornthwaite and sat at the top of the table. The Della Robbias looked tinny and cheap, their sorrow static, but I envied their stasis. I believed change exciting, an adventure, but I had simply moved from Simon to Ed. I no longer knew how to respond.

After a quarter of an hour a librarian I'd scarcely ever seen came in.

'That's who it is, we wondered.' She called to someone. 'It's Miriam, Miriam Henderson.' She turned back to me, 'Working?'

I pointed at the book I'd placed on the table as a pretext for being there. 'Finishing this.'

'We'll lock up after you've gone. There are no more seminars for this term.'

She went out. How did she know my name? I didn't know hers.

Hild

I knew it was me and Gray the minute I started reading it anyway she shouldn't have sent it round, Jeff said everything had to go to him so she did it on purpose so everyone would know and think me and Gray were splitting up. She doesn't deserve Ed, he's such a kind man, always looking after people, more than kind a really good man, a loving man. I tried to get to know her I tried to be friends with her, sending her little notes and buying her little presents and talking to her about her writing and the things she liked to talk about like books, and I tried to talk to her about her children because it must be difficult for her with Ed and all, they couldn't have been very happy about her leaving their father and going off with Ed, and Ed was left by Laura so it wasn't his fault, she left her husband, it was hers. But she wouldn't talk to me, it was as if I was not good enough to be talked to about her family or her work or anything, she thought she was better than the rest of us different. I'll say she was different she ate weird food and didn't like reading the same books or doing the things the rest of us liked, even someone so talented as Nicole much more talented than her liked being a normal human being, but she had to be different. And she wrote that story about me and Gray splitting up and made out it was all my fault. It was a lie. He came here with me. He'd never leave me. Whatever I did. I wasn't splitting up with him. It was her who'd split. And she didn't know anything about Ed. She didn't know how good he was. I went to see him the evening we'd been on the fells, Gray was out delivering late down to Millom, and it was thundering and I thought being with Ed would make me feel safer. I was right at the bottom of their stairs and I heard them having a row, well I heard her she was shouting, and I felt too frightened to go up and I felt sorry for Ed because he's such a good man.

And then after he started being my counsellor we spent such a lot of time together especially when his room was being redecorated. The painters took ages and he was mumpy about it so I made a special effort to tell him stories to take him out of himself, and we had to walk across the campus together and back, as well as having the counselling and I knew he was falling in love with me because I felt he wanted to hold my hand but wouldn't because everyone would see and he was too kind to do that to Miriam, so then I knew. I knew I had to save him from himself as he'd saved me. I wasn't going to take advantage of his love so I would leave uni. I didn't tell Gray that Ed was why I wanted to leave uni, I just said it was not the right course for me. This campus they were all tourism or agriculture students and sort of stick in the muds. And Gray went a bit quiet and then he said, it'd be alright, I always bounced back and we wouldn't go back to Leeds we'd go to Whitby because that was our home really in our hearts, it always had been. And Whitby had got some really interesting people in it for me to write about, more interesting than in this town because Whitby had got Dracula and tourists, and there was a college in Scarborough, he bet I could do my writing there if I wanted, and he'd get work easily because of the tourists. Poor Ed, he didn't know himself very well, he didn't know he was falling in love with me, but I can tell when my saviours started to fall in love with me even the women ones, they start to avoid my eyes as if to stop themselves being too attracted by them. And I knew I had eyes which were so blue it did attract men and women, they said they were innocent, and they would start saying they couldn't see me all the time because it might make people talk. That was when I knew I had to give them up. So I did. I gave up Ed for his own sake I couldn't let him go falling in love with me, it might have been bad for his career, and maybe me giving him up would show him he was too good for Miriam. Or maybe she'd see he was so good and she'd go back to being in love with him. But I don't think she was in love with him, ever. I didn't know why she was with him at all. Actually I hoped me giving up Ed would make him give her up, because he'd see what true love was, from me giving him up. And she didn't deserve him. This journal is ended now. I am starting a fresh chapter in my life, there's always a new beginning. It will be my new adventure by the sea with my prince. But I'll always be grateful for what Ed did for me. And Jeff and Francesca and Nicole. But mostly Ed.

Ed

Something must have made her write the story, but I couldn't work out what. Up until then she'd only written about her childhood and early life, at least that was what she told me. All I could think was she must have been jealous. Hild wrote quite well, and Miriam saw it, and finally recognised maybe she wasn't the writer she thought herself. But we have to accept our failures. No one her age – we are not old, but we aren't young either – makes a career out of writing. It was careless of her to send it to her writer's workshop. She said it was an accident, she was sending it to her brother. I don't know how she could have made such a mistake, unless . . . maybe she'd had a couple of drinks. If she had it could have been an accident, though Francesca didn't think it was.

Francesca was furious. I was very worried and annoyed. We'd had all the trouble with Hild going missing and getting herself into the paper, which we'd managed to resolve by putting Hild on the buddy scheme. Then Miriam started everything up again, sending a story which Hild thought libelled her and Graham – though Jeff didn't really think it did – and stole her life story, which might have been the case, but what did it matter, if, as Hild claimed, she wasn't going to write it herself? Rocks and geological time scales have their puzzles and intricacies, but they aren't complicated.

It was wonderful meeting Miriam, a new beginning. She told me she was writing, but I didn't find out how obsessed she was by it until Hild came on the scene. Except for her teaching, she was always vague about what she was doing.

Anyway, Francesca sorted it. At a meeting of the senior staff she indicated both women had to leave the campus, so to speak. The consensus was Miriam would not be offered another contract, but there was disagreement over Hild. Although she had shown herself to be very volatile she was a student, and the university – and particularly Jeff – couldn't really afford to lose her. And if she complained, and it got out, it would look bad. In the end we decided Hild would be offered an ultimatum. Concentrate on her studies or we would ease her transfer to another establishment. Francesca said she would interview both of them after we had got through the Union's Christmas party, the Ball, as Miriam and the students insisted on terming it, which promised to be problematic as we didn't want further histrionics to make matters worse.

Her writing. Maybe Miriam wasn't vague, but secretive. Perhaps it was a good thing to have happened, her story getting out and the ensuing fuss, perhaps it has taught her she can't really think of writing as a career.

Barn

The roof of the barn shimmers with ice crystals. On the ground, figures hurry in and out of the great wooden doors carrying trays of pies, baskets of bread, platters of cheese and cake. They wear snoods on their heads, checked trousers, clogs on their feet. Most are skinny, but some already have the large haunches which go with a life time of moving from chopping board to stove.

Outside, red flames rise from braziers. Around them, the yard is obscure, but the walls of the shippon and the barn waver in their light. By each brazier stand other figures, wrapped in coats, collars turned up, hats pulled low. Leaning on a fire beater, a bucket of water at their sides, they watch the heat.

Inside, lanterns dangle from the beams. Shafts of colour create a warm, glowing space. Bunches of holly and ivy hang on the walls, and wreathed portraits of strange beings. Pinheads of light entwined among them give glimpses of a wicked eye, a listening ear, a mocking mouth. An owl sits on the central truss. Its head turns, following the movement below.

Two spotlights are trained on the threshing platform, creating a stage, shadowy at the rear. The apron, behind low hurdles woven from green bay, is set with the pale discs of drums, the orange flashes of cymbals, and the metal spark of guitar strings. The lights merge on a square outlined in the floor.

A lone figure is here, garlanded with a wreath of ivy. The figure wears faded blue jeans. He, for the figure is male, plucks a violin, then fingers a lute, singing, 'Now the green blade rises', a strange rondel, foreboding and thrilling. Satisfied, he puts the instrument down and moves to the square in centre stage. His foot knocks on an iron ring. He stoops, pulls at the ring, slides a hatch to one side, and exposes the dark gape beneath.

He vaults from the stage, goes through the high doorway and softly hails two figures on guard at a brazier. The shorter one is bellied like the lute, the taller claps him on the back. He speaks, and the taller leaves his guardianship of the fire. Together they disappear around the end wall where the ground falls away and a door leads to the space under the hatch.

Through the yard gate come new arrivals. They are clad in strips of rag from the tops of their heads to their putteed shins. They wear heavy black work boots. Mummers. Carrying tambourine and drum they go towards a byre which abuts the barn. A whistle pipes a scale, a horn blares.

Vans and cars disgorge more figures. Goths in black with nose-studs, bikers wearing leather trousers and armlets. Girls clad in velvet gowns, men in kilts. Fauns. Elves. A bishop with gold crosier and mitre. All wear masks in indigo, emerald, vermilion. Jewels add glitter and gaiety. Swirling, not knowing who they greet, they shout to each other until the great doors suck them in and they jam four deep by the shippon, where sweaty cooks ladle out mugs of steaming ale. Wending their way back into the main barn they indulge in scuffles over straw bales. At last smaller bodies settle on the knees of bigger bodies. They drink and clamour, point wonderingly at painted faces half hidden in foliage.

Most vehicles go back the way they came, but four come to rest among a standing of nettles. To get out, the occupants clamber over gears and shuffle along back seats, their costumes dull, uniform, their masks not jewelled, the women Puritans in long grey skirts, shawls, bonnets, the men in sacks. Scarecrows with turnip features. Led by one scarecrow, eyes glinting through his hessian, this cohort, the Custodians, approach the building with determination. It seems they are obliged to attend. Yet, emerging from the shippon with brimming mugs, their mouths curve below their masks and they too are seen to laugh.

At first, so gently only the owl swivels its head, over the banter, the squeals, comes a vibration. It is the tune earlier plucked on the lute, now played on a fiddle. Up through the hatch rises the ivy-crowned fiddler, a cloak of leaves hanging from his shoulders. He plays louder, faster, sways and concludes. Clasping the violin in his right hand, he leaps to the front of the stage. The revellers, silenced earlier by his exhilarating sound and the figure's wildness, clap and catcall. The fiddler's bow sketches his thanks in the air. He begins another tune. Some get to their feet to dance with an abandon they didn't know they possessed. Others join them. They dance on. After half an hour he strums a song to its finish, picks up a stick and hits the cymbal a ringing blow. It is time to eat.

Donning heads fashioned into the likeness of goat and deer, hare and fish, the servers come from the shippon holding trays. Guests again tussle for the straw bales, reach out to snatch tranches of bread laden with spiced delicacies and pastries. The Custodians take their victuals, their patrol recognised and ignored. No one sees the fiddler replace the hatch.

Part way through eating, a tambourine rattles and taps. Ragcoats doffed, mummers enter clad in blue. Close-fitting caps cover their hair, features are erased by tight masks. Eyes, noses, mouths slashed in, they are spectral.

They shamble, arms dangling, boots thumping, and sing, 'Oh we shall go a-mummering amongst the fields so green'. The carousers gawp. Cries of 'I know who . . .' fade away. Legs stuck out to trip them are pulled back, the owners afraid of crossing these apparitions. The whistle shrills, the mummers don tabards. Devil Doubty ceremonially names the players. The Turkish Knight and St George feint with their swords, St George is killed, the King of Egypt's daughter swoons. About them frolics Devil Doubty, a head higher than the rest, and at his heels a mummer copies his every lewd caper. The doctor forces a potion down St George's throat. St George comes back to life and marries the King of Egypt's daughter. The mummers wind their way around the floor singing, 'We all want some figgy pudding so bring some out here.'

Applause is curtailed as the Master Cook bellows, 'Figgie puddins! Come and get 'em.' There is a scramble. Pies scorch fingers, causing yelps of pain. More ale is poured. Some carry mugs to the braziers, some drank in the shippon. Behind them, greeted with cheers and boisterous laughter, a band gets underway. The owl launches itself from the rafter, calls once, calls twice.

And the sport commences . . .

'The mummers were weird, all dressed up in plastic.' I yelled, the music of the Peelers crashing about me, 'Why weren't they cloaked?'

'Jeff says these plays are weird.'

What was weirder than the play itself, I was unable to tell who you were. After nine months of knowing you, and after the past week, I should have thought myself capable of identifying you anywhere, even dressed in the pale blue operating scrubs – the same blue as your wedding dress –

with which Jeff had camouflaged the company.

Which of them, now joining the throng waving their mugs of steaming drink, were you? You had to be there and you couldn't be the very tall, cavorting Devil Doubty. Were you the shortest, the one aping him?

After my "slip-up" Francesca had dictated all the female staff wear the same drab costume like a bunch of puritans, insisting on dowdy anonymity, with the male staff as scarecrows, so we were recognisable if there was trouble. I didn't have to comply, but I did.

Yet Francesca had achieved a miracle. Reception and Nicole, who witnessed the scene you made, said nothing. Astonishingly – despite the apology I had to send I expected you to broadcast my theft – you said nothing either, and if it wasn't for what had happened, I could have abandoned myself to the evening. The ball felt a success. Though the costuming wasn't what I imagined, the food was delicious, the wassail spicy. Chris Juste's playing revealed a new side to folk dancing, The Peelers were belting out their rock with crude energy, the students partying with zest.

I leant in to Ed, 'Do you want to dance?'

Ed spread his hands.

I bawled, 'Want to dance?' and did a couple of steps.

Not able to make out whether he did or not, I squeezed onto the dance floor to where a girl was spinning round, one arm raised to the rafters, the other indicating a voluptuous hip. Ed looked baffled, but followed. She started to undulate. I couldn't hear the jingle of the belt tied around her waist, but through the chiffon of her skirt her buttocks shimmied, and above her shaking belly her tasselled nipples trembled. She was expert.

I looked beyond her to where the mummers circled round and round, hands gripping each other's shoulders.

It was a victory rite, celebrating their performance. In the middle, well above the throng, I could see the cap of the very tall mummer bobbing up and down. It had to be Jeff, all the others were so much less tall. I tugged Ed's sleeve and mouthed, "Jeff"? Ed nodded. Because of his mask, it was difficult to tell what he was thinking, whether he was smiling. I hoped he was. I hoped his fears were allayed by the noise and the feeling of cheerfulness which oozed through the crowd like a dollop of syrup.

Ed wasn't a good dancer, but once he warmed up, he was wholehearted. All I could do was dance alongside his eccentricity, avoiding his arms and legs as they shot out to a rhythm of his own. A huge perspiring Superman and a petite fairy nudged each other. He had been identified. Now they would all recognise him.

The mummers broke ranks to twirl more and more people into their ring, the tallest blue cap continuing to dip and rise on its own. At the moment Ed achieved his most extravagant move, one of the mummers, the shortest, appeared at his side. It snatched for his hand. It pulled him – it was an abduction – towards the ring. Propelled into its centre, Ed and Jeff met. Shiny blue and turnip-featured scarecrow head tapped in cod-greeting then wove past each other, tracing knots on the floor, while the rest of the troupe tramped their way around them.

'Lost him.' Chris Juste stood beside me. A cloak of bay dangled from a leather lace around his neck. He'd made it from some of the leafier branches I'd set aside for the braziers. Cutting through the scent of the food and the smoke which drifted in through the barn doors and lay in layers above our heads, he smelled peppery and fresh.

'Lost?'

'Dr Gallagher – he's unmistakeable, like the man

he's dancing with, the one from the picnic, what's his name?' Despite the level of the band I could hear him easily.

'Jeff Young. Why are they unmistakeable?'

'Jeff Young is taller than most people here–'

'You're right.'

'And Dr Gallagher is uncoordinated.'

'No, he isn't.'

'Well then he's coordinated in a different degree.'

'Do you know who I am?'

'Reckon so, a woman staff member about the same height as me, dancing with Dr Gallagher, has to be Miriam Henderson.'

'Have you heard that it's bad luck to unmask a guiser?'

'You aren't a guiser, and I haven't unmasked you – simply recognised you.'

'So we aren't well disguised then?'

'Are you supposed to be? Dance? I'm playing soon.'

'Yes.'

He plunged to one of the barrels used for glass collection, put his mug down, and, scattering bay leaves, plunged back. He pulled me free of the bystanders and on to the floor. It was even more crowded, the dancers pushed to the margins by the mummers and their recruits. A number of doubly absurd pairings had happened. A faun clasped a biker to his chest, and a girl in a tutu clinched an elf in a pointy hat.

Chris jostled us some room. After a minute he shouted at me, 'You're good.' There was no surprise in his voice.

'So are you.'

'Should be, as a musician, though it doesn't always follow. Where'd you learn?'

'Argentina. I grew up there.'

'You speak Spanish?'

'Not now – or rather not as fluently now. I haven't been back for years.'

'I'd like to go to South America. I've never been anywhere except France and Greece.'

'Go now, while you're unencumbered.'

'What do you mean?'

'While you've got no ties.'

'Already tied to my music. Freelance musicians can't afford to take time off.'

'What was it you were playing at the beginning?'

'French carol – resurrection.' His yell coincided with the final crash of the Peelers last number and the word "resurrection" came out at top volume. The lone belly dancer giggled, her undulation slowed, her arms dropping to her sides.

'It's about love being reborn. Sorry got to go, I'm on. Great dancing.'

He shoved through the horde, who stroked the leaves of his cloak as if they were a charm, inhaling the scent from their hands.

The belly dancer said 'What a nice boy,' the words making her veil flutter. Despite the irony I could see longing in her eyes through the fringe of coins hanging low over her brow and cheekbones.

'Go after him.'

She turned and waded into the crowd, slapping away the hands which attempted to stroke her as she passed.

I looked around. Jeff was on the floor, but Ed had disappeared. Then I saw him going into the shippon, followed by a mummer, and I was pretty sure it was the abductor. Sure it was a "she", not a "he". Convinced the "she" was you, I started to follow. Chris was right. Ed lacked coordination. He was ungainly, as Jeff – the same height as him – was not, and it made him defenceless.

At the great door, two female staff in puritan shawls and bonnets were scanning the crowd. They saw me and beckoned. I pretended I hadn't seen them and continued to fight through to the shippon. By the time I reached it there was no sign of Ed, or you. In the crush, orders of beer, cider and wine were whizzed at the bartenders, who sashayed around at impossible speed handing out slopped glasses. Identified by my costume I was served at once. Turning to go, I noticed the signpost behind the bar directing the flow of drinkers. A green man astride an arrow. The drawing was crude but vigorous, the face comical. But it wasn't an arrow, it was his pizzle. It made me aware, as I struggled past the divers clowns, bullfighters, gymnasts who lined the wall that, though they sucked in their stomachs, even so I managed to rub, elbow and press against all of them.

Back in the barn the mood had altered. Chris had started his middle set. Under the influence of his voice the partygoers were taking a break. They lolled on the straw bales listening, while the belly dancer lay supine before Chris with the air of a devotee. I couldn't see Ed anywhere. Perhaps he'd gone back with the mummers to the byre, where they could uncover and drink without betraying themselves. Then one of the female patrol re-entered the building and in the less frenetic atmosphere I was not able to avoid her summons.

I picked my way among those dancers who had failed to gain the straw bales. They had swept bracken into mounds and lounged on it back to back, transforming their bodies into the shape of a writhing dragon.

Before I reached the grey puritan, I met Jeff.

'Have you seen Ed?'

Instead of answering, he asked, 'Who, dear lady, are you?' It didn't sound like Jeff, strangled by its headgear, but I was sure it was his voice.

'Don't be unreasonable, Jeff. If a musician I scarcely know can tell who I am, you must be able to.'

'But does the musician want to know you?'

'What are you implying?'

'Nothing – but it proves my point. How do you "know" who I am?'

'You are Devil Doubty and you're so tall you have to be Jeff.'

He laughed. 'Neither you nor I can be sure of anything. Devil Doubty can be man or woman. I could be the devil himself. You could be – anyone.'

'You must be Devil Doubty. Everyone else is too short.'

In response the figure gave me a deep ambiguous flourish – though there was no ambiguity, it was intended to deride – said, 'Who is this Ed you talk of?' and walked off with a swagger which unsettled me.

'Where's Ed?' The female staff member accosted me.

'I just asked Devil Doubty that.'

Was it Nicole? After Jeff's challenge, I was uncertain. We hadn't spoken since her phone call, and I was thrown by her brusqueness.

'I've not seen him since we were dancing. Or, rather, not since he went to the bar.'

'Perhaps he's with the mummers,' she said.

'I thought Jeff wanted to keep them in seclusion.'

She was definite. 'Not from Ed.'

'No? Jeff's keen on certain aspects of tradition.'

'But not the costume. They look like something out of a terrorist camp.' Only Nicole would make such a comparison.

'I expect he'll be back soon – Watersmeet are on next.'

'That's why Francesca wants Ed – to turn the volume down.'

'It's too late – they did the sound check before the ball started. They won't change the levels now.'

The puritan gestured with exasperation and turned to go.

'When you first put forward a masked ball I didn't understand how pointless, unless one was intent on predatory flirtation, it could be. This isn't a Christmas party, it's a futile attempt at Saturnalia.'

It was Nicole. What she said was a rebuke. From her? It wasn't like Nicole to disapprove. From Francesca? The rebuke must be from Francesca, but Nicole relayed it, so it was from her as well. All of a sudden my confidence in the evening disintegrated. The ball was a ceilidh, a barn dance, as Ed said. The behaviour wasn't bacchanalian. It was a silly idea from a silly mind, as silly as he'd implied when he said I was hysterical.

There was a discordant jangle. The mummers entered playing follow-my-leader. They had covered themselves entirely in strips of coloured rag. As Chris announced that his set would finish with a dance, I caught sight of Ed. He had arrived in front of the stage with four young women in tight trousers, high heels, and frilly shirts. Watersmeet. They were masked with dramatic sweeps of eyeliner. The look was a cross between androgyny and the unsubtle femininity of the chorus line. Juxtaposed with Ed's scarecrow sacking the effect might have been laughable, but from the way he bent towards them I could tell he found them endearing. They were agreeing with what he said. One of them shot a cuff to look at a watch. In itself unusual, the action revealed she, at least, was not a woman.

The band left and Ed searched around for someone. I waved, but in the influx of people onto the dance floor Ed didn't see me. I tried to push my way to him, but the line of mummers, led by the shortest one, the abductor, met him and swallowed him up.

. . . Not the King of Egypt's daughter. Not Devil Doubty. Devil Doubty's Ape. The Abductor.

No longer the Abductor. The Seducer.

She dances as Salome might have done when she solicited the head of John the Baptist, inscribing lascivious circles with her hips, making her coloured rags flip and coil like snakes. She twists about, now coming to the Scarecrow, now dancing away, her head turned in invitation over her shoulder. The Seducer dares the Scarecrow to follow yet all the time stays within the ring of the stamping, jingling Mummers.

The Scarecrow tries to dance, but he doesn't have the rhythm. The more he is provoked, the more he retreats. He turns this way, that. He tries to burst from the ring. He can't get out. Wherever he dashes, the Mummers link arms, press shoulder to shoulder, deny him.

The Seducer strokes a hand over her breast. The sign.

She steps forward, lifts her arms to the Scarecrow's head. Emboldened by the yells of the Mummers, the Seducer runs pliant hands down the masked face, down the neck, down the body, grasps at him. The Scarecrow parries the grasp.

The Seducer crouches and goes in again, her grasping more forceful but the Scarecrow's great hands fend her off. The encircling Mummers spur the Seducer on with shrill cries. One of them lifts a horn, blows it and they move in closer, closer, until the Seducer is thrust into the Scarecrow.

The Seducer snatches off her cap and mask, down her back a gush of silver hair. The crowd moans. The Seducer's laughter is triumphant. He is her trophy, the latest of her conquests. She rips off the Scarecrow's mask. The crowd gasps.

Her cry is clamorous, jubilant. She must leave this place. He loves her. Too much, too much.

A Puritan hurtles into the circle. The Mummers fall back, the silence expectant. With deliberation the Puritan removes her mask and bonnet. She steps forward, throws back her arm her fingers spread wide . . .

I whipped my hand three times across your face, once on either cheek, and then again. You stumbled, and fell on Ed who tossed you from him. Too late to halt my attack, he gripped my arm above the elbow, frogmarched me to the great door.

Jeff caught you, steadied you. You resisted, twisted away. He reached out, grabbed you, hauled you to the yard. You lurched onto the cobbles, hands outstretched.

Chris struck a single jarring note and started to play. He was wrong. It was not a resurrection tune. The minor key proclaimed a dirge. The dancers started to pound out the rhythm.

'That was a terrible thing to do.' Ed was shaking. 'Terrible.'

You claimed he was in love with you. You threatened him with disgrace. You assaulted him.

And I was to blame?

Ed stared at you, transfixed, as you thrashed on the ground like a mauled bird. The music and the stamp of dancing feet muted the screams coming from your mouth. The marks of my fingers were scored on your face.

You were still, your hands pressed into your eyes. A round-bellied figure in a thick coat came to you. Magda. She bent heavily and lifted your head from the cobbles, leant over and spoke to you. Pushing her away you rolled onto your side, your hands made into fists covering your ears. Magda knelt beside you, prised away your fists, talked. She levered you over. You heaved yourself to your knees, rocked, almost went down. Finally you were upright. Shielding you from our gaze Magda put her arm across your back and led you to where a van waited at the gate.

Graham. He had seen you, lashing back and forth.

Ed put his mouth to my ear, his lips touching me like a kiss. 'I hope she won't lay charges.'

The music's frenzy ceased. Far away, an owl called. Graham backed the van, crept forwards, backed. Everything was too slow. At last he jolted off down the lane.

'The university isn't going to re-employ you.'

'How do you know?'

'A meeting with Francesca.'

'You didn't tell me.'

'It was confidential.'

'Confidentiality has never stopped you before.'

'This is different.'

Did Graham know how it would end? Did he know about them, your saviours, the men who saved you? Is this how it always ended? A new enthusiasm, a revelation, a catastrophe. Running away. If you were crazy enough to believe Ed was your saviour and in love with you, what was I?

Endpaper

The presents for my children were wrapped and ready to go. Ed's suitcase was in the hall, waiting for the taxi to take him on the first part of his journey to New York and Christmas with Tom.

'What will you do if Hild does press charges?'

'She won't.'

'If she does?'

I shrugged. 'I'll say I was ridding myself of my brockenspectre.'

Was it one word or two? Did it have a capital letter?

Ed crossed his legs abruptly. 'Your Brocken spectre? I told you, Miriam. The day on Gowbarrow. A Brocken spectre is a person's shadow. It can't be a person. If you say Hild is your Brocken spectre and you were trying to get rid of her, people will think you are unbalanced . . .'

I stopped listening. That day on Gowbarrow. I'd seen my brockenspectre, and taken it as an omen of promise.

'They will think you're mad.'

'Hild's gone, Ed. She won't be coming back.'

Which was true. Ed didn't know it, but neither was I.

The flat felt bleak. It might be anywhere. In the uncurtained window I saw only me reflected in the black of the glass.

Photo: Stuart Atkinson

Caroline Moir was born in the Sudan and has lived and worked in places as far apart as Newfoundland and Syria, Italy and Argentina.

As a playwright she was commissioned to write *St Wilfrid of Ripon* 2009, by Ripon Cathedral, and by Kendal Community Theatre *A Passion for Kendal* 2012, *Lady Anne Clifford – a woman cast out* 2013, and *The Wednesday Play ~ the plot to kill Jesus* 2015. She was Literary Director for *Kendal Yarns Festival of New Plays* in 2016.

She has read her work for the BBC, at the Edinburgh International Book Festival, and at 'Aye Write' in Glasgow, and most recently at Lancaster LitFest 2019 and online with Yvonne Battle-Felton. She has a PhD in Creative Writing from Glasgow University.

Stories from *the swaying corridors of the wagons-lits: a memoir in story* have been published in print and online by Transmission, Muse, swampwriting, from Glasgow to Saturn, BRAND Spilling Ink/ Unbound Press. She is re-writing her first novel *Jemillia*, set in a future New Forest and Edinburgh, and has just completed *Hunting Jenet Nish*, set in British Columbia, the first of a historical trilogy.

The swaying corridors of the wagons-lits was long listed for the Cinnamon Literature Award in 2020.
Brockenspectre was shortlisted for the Sceptre Prize in 2013.